At her door almost an hour later, she took out her key with a grin.

"See, Sheriff Ross, what you've done for me? I'm approaching the ranks of responsibility. I must thank you, kind sir!" She stood on tiptoe, obviously intending to kiss his cheek.

But he turned his head and leaned down slightly. Her lips were as smooth and sweet as they looked, and the kiss was no short, chaste, first-time kiss after all.

When she pulled away, breathless, a wondering look on her face, she said, "I—think maybe after that…you could call me Honey and I could call you Dal…."

He took the key from her, opened the door, shoved her gently inside, and returned the key. "Lock the door behind you."

Dear Reader,

The Promise Romance® you are about to read is a special kind of romance written with you in mind. It combines the thrill of newfound romance and the inspiration of a shared faith. By combining the two, we offer you an alternative to promiscuity and superficial relationships. Now you can read a romantic novel—with the romance left intact.

Promise Romances® will introduce you to exciting places and to men and women very much involved in today's fast-paced world, yet searching for romance and love with commitment—for the fulfillment of love's promise. You will enjoy sharing their experiences. Most of all you will be uplifted by a romance that involves much more than physical attraction.

Welcome to the world of Promise Romance® — a special kind of place with a special kind of love.

Etta Wilson

Etta Wilson, Editor

No Limits on Love

Patricia Dunaway

Promise Romances®

Thomas Nelson Publishers • Nashville • Camden • New York

Published in Nashville, Tennessee, by Thomas Nelson, Inc. and distributed in Canada by Lawson Falle, Ltd., Cambridge, Ontario.

All of the characters and events in this book are fictitious. Any resemblance to actual persons, living or dead, or to actual events is purely coincidental.

Printed in the United States of America.

ISBN 0-8407-7378-1

Chapter One

Cara Morgan, her feet planted wide on the sand, stretched her arms and let the joy within her swell until she thought perhaps she'd float off. How marvelous that would be, to float up into the glorious, endless sky! She'd be able to see the ocean as the setting sun fired its waves, to take it *all* in...

"Oh, dear God, how can I thank you?" she whispered, knowing a moment of pure happiness that lit her soul like the rays of the sun. "To live here, not just come when I can squeeze it in...it's wonderful! Thank you!" She spun around and around, arms still outstretched, until she collapsed in a laughing, breathless heap on the cold, wet sand.

Suddenly she felt a hand on her shoulder, and her eyes flew open to see a man, his steady gray eyes anxious, crouching close beside her. "Are you all right, miss?"

Cara stared up at him for a long moment, taking in his black hair and dark, low brows, the clean spare lines of his serious face. *He looks like...like...* Her mind scampered around until it pounced. "Gregory Peck!"

"I beg your pardon?" He'd dropped to one knee and was so close now that the faint outline of a scar was visible, just to the side of his mouth. It was a very fine mouth, too, sort of chiseled-looking, but generous. "Are you all right?"

"I...of course," Cara said carefully, with enormous dignity. "What makes you ask?"

"Well, I was watching when you flung your arms out, and when you dropped I thought maybe you were sick," he said quietly, but with such undertones of strength that Cara thought he probably wouldn't need a microphone to announce a football game in a stadium. "Is anything wrong?"

Cara rose as gracefully as possible. She was a tall woman, and had never managed to completely master her long legs. As he held onto her arm and rose with her, she could feel his fingers through the fabric of her wool jacket. "Why, of course not, I was just...just practicing." She wasn't about to tell him she'd been talking to God...thanking Him for a job she loved and for allowing her to move here to the Oregon coast, her favorite place in the whole world.

"Practicing for what?" He still held her arm and was close enough to look down into her eyes.

She had very large, very brown eyes that laughed as easily as her mouth. But now they were serious, matching his own somber expression. "I...might try out for a play," she improvised. "There's a part for a crazy woman."

"I see." Looking as though he had no trouble believing she'd get the part, he said, "So you're an actress."

"You sound as though you disapprove."

"Do I? Sorry."

While thinking he was a sort of sour-pickle person, Cara noticed that a large, black dog was watching them and that the man wore a uniform. She giggled suddenly, a habit that overtook her when she was nervous. "Are you the dogcatcher? If you are, there's a likely candidate for you."

"I'm Sheriff Ross, Dallas Ross." The frown between

6

his eyes deepened. "And that dog belongs to my mother."

"Oh! Sorry." A regretful little sigh escaped her lips. Would she never learn to say the right thing? Except for his sober attitude, she couldn't remember meeting a more attractive man. Though not exactly handsome, there was that resemblance to Gregory Peck—when he was a lot younger, of course. She sighed again.

"Miss, are you sure you're all right?" His chiseled features hardened suddenly. "Are you on something?"

"You mean drugs? Sheriff Ross, I'll have you know I don't do and never have done drugs!" she sputtered, so agitated the big black dog took a couple of anxious steps toward her.

"All right, all right, but you'll have to admit, from the way you've been acting and the way you're dressed, it was a logical assumption."

His words were calm, but they irritated Cara, mostly because she'd heard them, or variations of them, before. She glanced down at the camouflage paratrooper's pants, Army green Yukon underwear top, and oversized Navy pea coat. The only new article of clothing she wore was a pair of Nike running shoes. Even the elaborately beaded, Indian headband that kept the gold-brown, curly mop of chin-length hair out of her eyes was from a second-hand shop called Yesterday's Gone. "Does that dog bite people?"

"Only if they deserve it, and he's smart enough to know who does and who doesn't." There was a hint of something, not quite humor, in his tone.

Cara put out her hand, palm down, and the huge dog sniffed delicately at it, his fine brown eyes meeting Cara's own wide brown ones. "He likes me," she said smugly.

"He hardly ever makes a mistake," he murmured, but the words carried no venom. "Well, ah...Miss..."

"Morgan, Honey Morgan." She extended her hand to him, wondering why she'd told him her dad's nick-

7

name for her. Ever since she could remember he'd called her Cara-Honey. The thought flew from her mind as Dallas Ross's hand, large and warm, held hers briefly, tightly, before he released it. In fact, she seemed almost hypnotized as she gazed up into his face. There was something about him…maybe she'd told him her nickname because she wanted to hear him say it…

Turning to the dog, he snapped his fingers. "Come on, Beau." He touched his hat and said, "Nice to have met you, Miss Morgan. Maybe we'll see you again."

He began to walk, his long, easy stride matched by the dog at his side, and because she couldn't bring herself to go in the opposite direction—which she needed to do to get home—Cara fell into step with them. "You exercise Beau often?"

He nodded. "My mother's out of town for a couple of months, and I'm keeping him for her."

"Have you lived here long?" she asked, thinking the man and dog were both lean and fit-looking.

"Most of my life. How about you? You aren't from around here."

She couldn't keep the smile from her lips. He was so serious his face seemed carved in stone. It made her want to make him laugh. "No, I'm from Venus." Now Cara knew very well that she didn't look like a love goddess, far from it. True, her eyes were big and velvety brown, with high, arched, expressive brows. Her nose was a bit snub, but not bad; her mouth, usually curved in a smile, had a full lower lip and a well-shaped upper lip. The bulky clothes she wore disguised the fact that she was every inch a female—but not quite in the same category as a love goddess. With a mischievous gleam in her eyes she added, "You don't believe I'm from Venus, huh?"

He glanced at her from head to toe. "You do look kind of alien in that getup. I'm about used to the fact that I don't see skirts much anymore, but that outfit…"

As he began walking again, Cara told herself it didn't

8

matter that they'd soon be two miles farther from her cottage. "I wear skirts. But the truth is, it's cold in October, and I like to walk on the beach, too. You try it in a skirt and see how you feel!"

"Arrested, probably, and the ex-sheriff of Tillicum," he said dryly. "Although these days the sexes seem to be getting mixed up."

"Oh, I hate that!"

A little startled by her vehemence, he asked, "What?"

"I like for men to be tall, dark, handsome men! And women…"

"Yes?"

"Glad of it," she finished, thinking he was very close to the trite but fascinating description—tall, dark, and handsome—and that he most likely thought she was close to certifiably nuts.

He nodded, but it was too dark to see the expression on his face as he said, "Are we near your house?"

"Nope, it's a couple of miles north."

"Then why did you walk so far out of the way?"

"I told you. I like to walk on the beach." She turned and started walking back the other way, but he caught up with her in a few quick strides and took her arm.

"Don't you know you shouldn't walk alone after dark?"

"I resent that!"

"You resent what? My concern?"

She drew away at the sound of his words. He was awfully serious and intense. Not that she didn't like it, just the opposite. Somewhere on a deep level that had gone largely untouched in her twenty-two years, she felt a stirring of strange excitement.

Keeping her husky voice low, she said, "No, not at all. I resent the fact that these days either a woman doesn't feel safe, or she really isn't. It's not fair."

"It may not be fair, but the facts are pretty clear. You shouldn't be out alone. You're old enough to use better judgment." He stopped and peered at her face in the dimness of the twilight. "How old are you, anyway?"

"Twenty-two, Sheriff. Are you on duty, or do you always appoint yourself guardian of any woman you come across?"

"Only the ones without the sense of a goose." His hand was firm on her elbow. "Come on, I'll take you home in the squad car. Give the neighbors something to talk about."

"That won't be anything new," she murmured, struggling to keep up with him as he walked in the loose sand near the path that led to the parking area. "This isn't necessary, you know."

"I'm not so sure, Miss Morgan. Seems to me you need someone to look after you."

"And you've appointed yourself?" she repeated a little sarcastically before she thought better of it. The idea wasn't exactly repugnant.

"The county appointed me and pays my salary to do just that."

"Oh, sure." Cara was silent as he opened the back door of the car and motioned for the dog to get in, then courteously helped her into the front. They didn't speak as he drove her back to where her rented house stood like a sentinel on the knoll above the sea, and for a moment she almost forgot him in her pleasure at seeing its snug outline.

Anyone who reads books about Scotland or Ireland or England, who pores over the pictures of the cunning country houses—as Cara did—would have said it could be at home in any of those places. It was well-proportioned, with a tiny porch, small-paned windows on either side of the door, and even a bay window on the left end. Someone with an imagination as fertile as Cara's had painted it the faintest pinky-cream and proclaimed it Rose Cottage on a carved wooden sign.

Cara could imagine what he would say when he found out she was staying alone.

She was right. After walking her to the door he said,

"I take it that you're not married, that you live here alone?" Disapproval was plain in his tone.

"Right. How about you, Sheriff? Are you married?"

"As a matter of fact, I'm not."

Why did she suddenly feel foolishly happy? "Then how about coming in and peeking under my bed?"

"I beg your pardon?" His expression was half-shocked, half-disapproving now.

"Oh, that's just what Mom always says when she comes home to an empty house. I guess she means check things out."

"Would it make you feel better?"

Thinking he had the deepest, nicest voice she'd ever heard in a man, Cara struggled to be independent and cool and tell him no. She lost and gave in to the desire to have him stay a little longer. "Um, would you mind?"

"Of course not. I told you, it's my job."

"Your job. Sure." She opened the door, stepped inside, and switched on the light all in one graceful motion.

"You mean you live here alone and you don't lock your doors when you go out?" He stood in the doorway, his scowl fierce.

"Sheriff Ross, it's obvious you don't approve of me. I'm sorry—but not too much." With a grin she added, "I'm going to have some cider. It was chilly out there. Want some?"

He looked as though a struggle were going on in his mind, as he watched her poke at the gently burning fire in the red brick fireplace. She added a couple of logs, making the cozy room almost irresistible. "I am off duty," he said slowly.

"You could have fooled me." Cara hung her pea coat on a peg near the kitchen door and went to the refrigerator. She took out the jug of cider, put a pot on the tiny stove, and then stood waiting. "Well?"

"Well what?"

"Do you want cider or not? It's not hard, if you're a

11

teetotaler." She giggled suddenly at a memory. "Once we kept some too long and it got…um, sort of fizzy. Jill and I poured it into the gutters and the gulls drank it. They got really silly. Want some?"

As though he still weren't sure, he nodded and sat down in a big, dark red, plush chair that looked as though it might be comfortable even for a man his size. *It is,* Dallas thought, as he looked around at the room. Cara poured the cider and disappeared.

The cottage was old. An oriental rug covered most of the wood living room floor. Still vibrant with color, its dull red, muted gold, and soft blue on a beige background were echoed in the chair in which he sat, and in the old-soldier blue of the chair opposite him. The lamps had a mix of fringed and tasseled and cut-paper shades, and the light they gave was pleasant. On either side of the fireplace were glassed-in bookshelves filled to capacity with hardbound books. There were no paperbacks; at least none was visible. As far as he could see, everything in the room was at least forty or fifty years old, and it gave him a curious feeling.

Cara came back in just then, and he noticed she'd changed her clothes. The dress she now wore was of soft blue cotton, and the waist of it was nearer her hips. The fresh, wide white collar framed her face, and her wavy hair looked as though it might crackle.

"You look…" he stopped. At her questioning expression he said, "You look old. No, I mean you remind me of my grandmother—"

"I *what?*"

"I didn't mean that the way it sounded. Actually, when she was your age my grandmother was a very pretty woman," he hastened to add. "It's just that this room, your dress, your hair—it all makes me feel as if we've stepped back fifty years in time."

"Really? That's great!" She smiled delightedly as she gave him a thick white trucker's mug. The fragrance of steaming cinnamon and cloves perfumed the air. Carefully keeping her own mug upright, she sat in the blue chair opposite him, one bare foot tucked beneath her, the other tapping the floor impatiently as she blew on her cider.

"I take it you don't care for new things."

"You are exactly right. Either someone gives them to me, or I buy my clothes in second-hand stores. The same is true of my books, and my furniture, too, what there is of it. Not everyone likes old stuff." She took a delicate sip, then asked, "How about you?"

His hands wrapped around the comforting warmth of his mug. "I never thought much about it. My apartment's furnished—"

"You mean you don't have your own things?" she asked, as though nothing could be worse.

"A bachelor doesn't need much."

"Even a bachelor needs an identity!"

The frown had returned. "Miss Morgan—"

"Call me Honey," she said, watching him from beneath her lashes.

"I was about to say, a person's identity comes from other things besides possessions."

"Sure, but what you surround yourself with can clue people in to who you really are, don't you think?"

"I suppose, but if you didn't want people to know you, wouldn't it be easy to deceive them?"

"Sheriff, what kind of friends do you have? Or are you talking about yourself?"

He missed the teasing edge in her question and answered seriously. "Remember, I'm a law officer, and more often than not people do try to hide things from me."

Cara's laugh rang out. "Sheriff Ross, you're as tight as the bark on a sycamore tree! You need someone to loosen you up."

He drained the mug and put it down on the small table beside his chair as he stood up, his face set. "I suppose you think you could do it."

"Piece of cake." She snapped her fingers, then added

13

with a grin, "I can do the job at least as well as you can take care of me. Why, you haven't even peeked under my bed—"

"I'd best be going. Thanks for the cider."

"Any time," said Cara, rising to her feet as he went to the door, thinking it wasn't likely he'd be dropping in any time soon for cider. She'd probably have to break the law before the sober-sided sheriff came around again. Her little grin appeared again. It might be worth it!

At the door he paused to examine the flimsy lock. "This is useless even if you took the trouble to use it."

"Really? Then, maybe you ought to leave Beau with me."

"A dog isn't a bad idea, and you ought to take these things more seriously." His tone was nothing short of severe.

"Well, I do have an attack cat, sir," she said, but the meekness she tried so hard to put into her words melted away. "Sheriff Ross, you're fighting a lost cause with me. I just trust people. Why would anyone want to harm me?"

Once again the scowl on his face grew fierce. "Miss Morgan—"

"Honey."

"You're a young woman living alone, and if you don't wake up and realize that there's an ugly element in our society, you might find out the hard way."

Cara couldn't think of a thing to say to that, so she just nodded and watched him stride toward his car, his exasperation plain even in his walk.

She sighed as she closed the door and locked it dutifully after his taillights disappeared. At least he'd said she looked like his grandmother, and she'd been pretty. But a few moments later when she went out to get more wood for the fire, she forgot his dour warning, and left the door unlocked as usual.

Chapter Two

"So, Cara, how has your first month on the job gone?" Mrs. Lane, the county supervisor for Senior Services, had a pleasant smile on her broad, smooth face, but Cara wasn't fooled. In spite of the fact that Cara had excellent references, the woman had resisted hiring her. She had thought Cara was too young.

"Very well, Mrs. Lane," Cara said with an answering smile that covered her anxiety. She sat a bit straighter as she glanced around the cluttered office, feeling less intimidated. Obviously Mrs. Lane didn't always get everything done, either.

Mrs. Lane riffled through the papers on her desk and looked up as she found Cara's file. "Am I to understand that Bessie Greenstreet recommended you?"

"Yes, that's true. She was a lifelong friend to my grandmother, and I worked for her almost two years."

"And several others of her acquaintance, I gather."

Cara nodded. "My mother started her job when I went to school, and when my grandmother came to live with us—I was almost twelve at the time—I enjoyed caring for her."

"What exactly were your duties?"

"My grandmother had a kind of diabetes that made it impossible for her to live alone, so I made sure she didn't hurt herself, that she took her medication, and I helped her weigh her food, those kinds of things."

"And her friends that you worked for?"

"Oh, I ran errands and did little chores around the house—their correspondence, the dishes, the beds, the dusting. You name it, I did it!" Cara finished with a little laugh.

Mrs. Lane cleared her throat, resisting Cara's levity. "I see. Very much like what you're doing now, it seems." She scanned a sheet in the file and said, "You fit all the requirements. A nurse's aide course, work experience, an aptitude for the job…"

Everything but maturity, right? thought Cara. "You've read my reports, then?"

"Of course." She smiled a little now. "I know how hard your job is, young woman, because I've done it. I see you've noted Ladell Abernethy's appetite is poor."

Cara hesitated. Miss Abernethy was one thorny problem she wasn't quite sure she could solve, at least not yet. Then she said honestly, "I get the feeling she's testing me, Mrs. Lane, and that if I don't give up, if I keep trying, she'll come around."

"You're probably right. And how about the Stewarts?"

The expression on Cara's face showed no trace of her earlier anxiety or unsureness now. "They're wonderful! Mrs. Stewart is still limited in what she's able to do, but Mr. Stewart is doing great with the cooking lessons."

"Cooking lessons?"

Too late, Cara remembered that she hadn't intended to mention her little project until she knew it was going to work. "Um, yes, I'm teaching him to cook. He makes a great omelet now, and we're working on soup."

The woman surprised her. "That sounds like a good idea, Cara. Now about Virgil Penhollow and Seretha Hodges."

"Seretha…ah, Mrs. Hodges, hasn't come back from that bout with the flu as well as I'd hoped. And I'm kind of worried about Mr. Penhollow because he refuses to go back to the doctor."

Mrs. Lane had been watching Cara closely as she spoke. "You like your job very much, don't you, Cara?"

"I do, Mrs. Lane, I really do. It's neat to get paid a salary for doing what I've done for spending money since I was fourteen."

"Yes, neat." Mrs. Lane deliberately made her face serious. "But you should realize the funds might be cut next year and we wouldn't be able to pay you for even the twenty-five hours a week that we do now. That's something else I wanted to ask you about. You don't have to tell me, of course, but you are young and I've been wondering about how you're managing."

Cara could see the woman's concern was genuine. "To tell the truth, I used up most of my savings when I moved. There's a little left, but I'm either going to have to move or get another part-time job."

"Really? What did you have in mind?"

"Well, I did waitress work while I was still in high school, and it wasn't too bad." Her brown eyes had a mischievous glint now. "After a while I hardly ever spilled things on people."

"That was a blessing, I'm sure," the older woman murmured. "I'll try to arrange at least five more hours for you."

"I'd appreciate that." Cara rose, not willing to tell Mrs. Lane she often worked that and many more above her allotted time already.

Mrs. Lane rose too and said slowly, as though she were still surprised, "From all the reports I've been getting, you're doing a fine job, Cara."

"Thanks. I enjoy it a lot, and I love all my people."

Completely thawed now, Mrs. Lane said, "I really believe you do, and that's the main requirement for this job. It's not an easy one."

Cara was carefully smoothing dark brown kid gloves on each hand. "I've always gotten along great with

17

older people. My grandma Naomi had lots of friends, and they always acted like I was one of the bunch. One of them, the Mrs. Greenstreet you mentioned, has a sister who lives here in Tillicum."

"We'll see you at the monthly staff meeting, then?"

"Sure. Thanks again, Mrs. Lane."

"For what, Cara? You're a good employee." She watched Cara straighten the richly patterned paisley scarf tied Gypsy-style around her head and shrug into her fur jacket. "A bit…um…unorthodox in your dress, but not improper, I suppose." As Cara left, Mrs. Lane shook her head, but there was an indulgent smile on her face.

Driving down the highway a little while later, and reveling in the view of the bay and the ocean beyond, Cara thought with an inward sigh that she would probably have to give up the little house. Much as she loved it, the rent was too high, after all. The idea of getting an apartment where she couldn't see the ocean was almost like a physical pain.

She wondered suddenly where Dallas Ross's apartment was and if *he* had a view of the ocean. Firmly pushing the image of his lean, somber face out of her mind, she conscientiously reviewed what she needed to do at Seretha Hodges's, for that was where she was heading.

Cara braked in front of Seretha's charming old house and thought with gratitude that although she often found it difficult to make friends of her own age, she'd made a friend of Seretha already.

She was waiting as usual, with tea brewed in the fine Staffordshire pot, alongside a rack of toast. "You're late, dear."

Her bright blue eyes watched as Cara carefully peeled off her gloves and hung up her fur jacket, a gift from Seretha herself, to reveal an interesting costume. The dark brown walking skirt didn't quite reach Cara's slender ankles, and her muted brown and gold calico blouse had puffy sleeves and a high, close neck. Her British tan riding boots, obviously used aplenty by a woman who once rode seriously, were polished to a high gloss. "That's a nice outfit you have on, Cara."

"Do you like it?" She twirled around, the bright smile on her expressive face lighting the entire room.

"Yes, but sit down before the tea gets any colder. You're supposed to be here by ten." She tried to speak severely, but the affection crept in despite her resolve. "Cara, being late is a discourtesy you can't afford."

"Yes, ma'am." She reached over and patted the old woman's wrinkled, age-spotted hand. "I apologize, and I'll do better. What kind of jam do we have? Any orange marmalade?"

"You know very well you ate all of it last week."

Cara made a wry face. "Oh dear, did I eat *all* of it?"

"You bought some strawberry to replace it, remember? And after all, you're a growing girl."

"Oh, I sincerely hope not!" Cara took the rose-sprigged cup of Earl Grey tea and spread the strawberry jam very, very thinly on her toast. She was fully aware that she'd have to make this time up later but was even more aware of how important it was to Seretha.

"So tell me, what's new in your life?"

The question was not an idle one. Cara knew that Seretha looked forward to hearing about the least happening in her life. "Well, I met a man a couple of days ago," she began, knowing this was the very kind of thing Seretha loved to hear. It was the kind of thing she'd not been able to tell, either, because Cara's love life was practically nonexistent. She had a habit of putting men off, saying the wrong thing at precisely the right time.

"A man?" Seretha feigned nonchalance, but Cara could see the bright interest. Though she was barely five feet tall, her lined face was carefully made up and her white hair twisted regally high. With her favorite rose and cream afghan tucked about her knees, she sat in her favorite chair as erectly as if it were a throne. "A nice respectable man, I trust?"

"Do you consider the sheriff nice and respectable?"

"You mean John Ross's boy?" Her brows raised delicately. "Fine family. John was a deacon, and Dallas has the makings of one. He's a fine young Christian man, yes."

"I don't know about his daddy's name being John, but he has black hair and gray eyes and a black dog big enough to ride."

"That's Dallas. Did you go out with him?" Seretha's blue eyes shone.

"No, he just took me home and lectured me about walking alone on the beach after dark and leaving my door unlocked—" Too late she saw Seretha's disapproving look.

"Cara, dear, you know he's right."

She didn't know any such thing. To be in constant fear that someone might harm her seemed to be a terrible way to live. But she held her peace, finished her tea, and said, "What else would you like me to do today besides the laundry and straightening up? Umm, how about beef barley soup for your lunch?" From the simplest routine housekeeping chores to shampooing hair, even giving permanents, back rubs, or pedicures, the list of things Cara did was endless. She provided whatever each old friend needed or wanted.

"That's it for today, and beef barley soup sounds wonderful." She hesitated, then said, "Cara, dear, are you sure you don't mind doing my lingerie by hand?"

As she gathered up the lovely old tea set, Cara said, "You know I don't mind. Your things are far too fragile and pretty to put in the washing machine."

"You're an unusual young woman, you know that?"

Just before she went through the door that led to the kitchen, Cara said, "Why? Because I like old clothes and don't lock my doors?" She hastened to add, "But I'm going to start; honestly, I am!"

"You'd better. And no, not because of your clothes. I like them." She cocked her head to one side. "Because you don't mind doing things for people that some would call low jobs. We've discussed it, and all of us think—"

"That even if Cara's a little spacey, she'll wash your underwear?"

"Oh, go on and do the dishes! And be careful that you don't break anything."

"You know I never break things." In spite of her scatterbrained reputation, she rarely broke anything. *And how fortunate,* thought Cara as she began the ritual of washing up. The house was a lovely melange of possessions, some very valuable, others valuable only for sentimental reasons.

Seretha was a widow, and although she had been born and raised in the area, she was the only one of her brothers and sisters left. She had a son who lived in Portland, but Cara had begun to suspect that for all of Seretha's fond talk of him, the man actually showed very little concern for his mother. It was for him, however, that Seretha was determined to save the valuable antiques and furniture, especially the German-made square grand piano which stood in the corner of the front room. Because Seretha often asked her to play it, Cara had just about overcome her awe of it.

Hands immersed in sudsy water halfway up to her elbows, Cara was daydreaming her way through the comforting, homely task. The view of the ocean from Seretha's kitchen window was heartbreakingly beautiful, but try as she might she couldn't block out the memory of the meeting with Sheriff Dallas Ross, guardian of the righteous.

"He'll ask you out." Seretha's words came floating into the spacious, well-planned kitchen, into her consciousness.

"Oh, I don't think so," Cara answered, knowing exactly whom Seretha meant and not bothering to try to fool her into thinking otherwise. "He seems like the kind of man who likes his women conventional." She dried her hands and went to stand in the doorway. "He didn't approve of me at all, I could tell."

The smile on Seretha's face was shrewd and knowing. "You're a pretty woman, and pretty women are hard to come by in a town this size. He and Janet Moody dated for what seemed like forever, but then she went off on some kind of mission tour to Africa."

"Oh, he has a girl—"

"He'll ask you out. What are you going to tell him?"

Cara shrugged her shoulders. "We aren't really suited at all. He's awfully serious, and I'm—"

"You're a bit flighty, but delightfully flighty, dear. This is going to be interesting." Seretha's expression showed just how much she looked forward to what she obviously considered an interesting development. "Who's next on your list today?"

"Virgil Penhollow," answered Cara absently.

Seretha nodded. "Cara, dear, before you go, could you play 'Smoke Gets in Your Eyes'? You seem to have a feel for the old songs. And…maybe we could do the Strauss waltzes together again? I love duets."

Cara went to Seretha and hugged her. "Sure we can. I love duetting with you!"

It was almost noon when she arrived at Virgil's. He'd told her he was born in a small hamlet just south of Tillicum, and for all of his seventy-six years had lived no farther away than thirty miles in any direction. A good many of those years had been spent on board a fishing boat on his beloved ocean.

Virgil and Cara shared several likes and dislikes, the sea being just one of their many likes. And though he never said it, Cara knew that in Virgil's mind she was the granddaughter of his fantasies. There'd been an instant rapport between the young Senior Services worker and the old bachelor.

The neat stone house where he lived wasn't in the

same class as Seretha's by any means, but he was just as adamant about not leaving it. As Cara made her way down the winding path that led to his home, she knew she'd somehow have to manage to get some repairs done before winter set in. The roof on the kitchen side had a small leak, and one pane of the front window needed replacing. Just then she saw his face at that window, and she knew he'd been watching for her. He didn't go out much anymore, except to walk on the beach and garner the ocean's harvest. Virgil Penhollow's heart condition was sapping his strength, his very life.

"Come in here, girl," he said from the door now. "It's getting mighty raw out there, you know."

"I know," she said, laughing as she stomped her feet on the sandy, scruffy old welcome mat. "Have you had lunch?"

"Not yet. Thought maybe we'd eat together."

Cara didn't waste time. As she passed through the living room, she picked up a small plate with a nibbled-on piece of toast and a half-full mug of coffee. "Virgil, is this all you had for breakfast?" she called back from the kitchen.

"No appetite, girl. But don't the women like lean men?"

"Lean, yes, but not skeletal!" The rattle of dishes punctuated her words. "Got some stuff for chowder?"

"Matter of fact, there are some clams. I dug 'em this morning. No milk, though, and not an onion on the premises." He leaned against the door frame.

Cara glanced back at him. He must have been a fine figure of a man when he was younger. His hair was a clear, light gray, the kind of gray a lot of black-haired people get as they age. His eyes were still very dark below his bushy gray brows, and his face was leathery from many hours in the sun and salt spray. He must have, at one time, looked a great deal like that Dallas Ross. Annoyed because he seemed to pop into her mind more often than their brief encounter warranted, she said, "I'll get these dishes done and chop the clams; then I'll run down to my place and get some milk. It's closer than the store."

"Pshaw, you don't have to go to all that trouble, Cara."

She noticed, and not for the first time, a grayish tinge to his skin, a pinched look around his eyes. "Sure I do. You've got clams, I've got milk and onions, I'm hungry, and it's lunch time!"

"I guess you're right," he said with a chuckle.

Fifteen minutes later Cara wheeled her little Ghia into her driveway, only to see another car parked there. She met Sheriff Ross as he came down the rocky path, a brown paper bag in his hand, a rather sheepish look on his face.

"You aren't home," he said.

"An astute observation, Sheriff," she said smiling at the grave look on his face, "one that speaks well for your powers of deduction."

"Miss Morgan, I get the impression that not only do you have an amazing disregard for your personal safety, but you also seem bound to insult my profession."

Cara's smile blossomed into a grin, then a healthy giggle. "Oh, for heaven's sake, lighten up! You don't even have a uniform on."

"It's my day off."

She stifled the giggle and walked past him to her door, then turned back. "And you came here to—"

He held up the paper bag. "I just happened to have a couple of extra dead-bolt locks."

"And you thought of my poor flimsy locks! I'm touched, Sheriff."

"Miss Morgan, you seem to have this urge to make fun of me."

Instantly Cara grew serious. Her lower lip caught in her teeth, she stared into his face. "You thought I was laughing at you."

"Weren't you?"

"Oh, no, you're wrong. I really am touched. This is my first time to live so far away from my family, and it's …it's nice to have someone care."

"Then you wouldn't mind if I installed these?"

Again she chewed her lip for a moment, then finally said, "Don't get me wrong; it's a good idea. But this is not a good time."

"Not a good time to be safe?"

"Oh, you always twist around what I say! I didn't mean that at all. The truth is, I can't afford it right now, and that's all there is to it."

"I told you I had these on hand. Did you hear me mention money?"

Cara shook her head, the gold curls bouncing emphatically. "I don't take things I can't pay for. I appreciate your thinking of it, believe me. Maybe in a couple of weeks."

"But—"

"But me no buts, Sheriff. That's the way I operate." The thought of Virgil waiting for her made her say, "I'm really sorry, but you'll have to excuse me. Thanks for the thought." She smiled brightly, a little embarrassed at having to admit her financial state, then disappeared into the house. A couple of minutes later she came out, a carton of milk in one hand, two onions in the other. She waved the onions and said, "I hate to run off like this, but I've got an appointment."

He watched her run up the path to her car and drive away, then turned back to the house, shrugging as he made the decision to do exactly what he'd come for. He would install the dead-bolt locks, regardless of what she'd said. As he got out his tools, he wondered two things: if she was really as poor as she'd said, and to what kind of appointment one took two onions and a half gallon of milk

Thirty minutes later, Dallas knocked three times, then opened the door of his Uncle Virgil's house. He caught a delectable whiff of clam chowder—with plenty of onions—and was very much surprised to see Cara come out of the kitchen, a yellow calico apron covering much of her brown outfit.

"Sheriff Ross!" she exclaimed, wiping her hands on the apron. "What are you doing here?"

"I could ask you the same question."

"You could," she agreed, "but I asked you first."

"Look, Miss Morgan, Virgil's my uncle. I come here often, and I came today to fix the roof."

Before she could reply to this surprising bit of information, Virgil's voice came from the kitchen. "Come on in, Dal, and have some chowder! Cara may be young, but she cooks like she was born in a galley."

"Be right in," Sheriff Ross called out, but to Cara he said, "How in the world do you happen to be here cooking lunch for my uncle?"

"Well, I—" Cara was saved from having to explain by another firm summons from Virgil.

"You two, come on, before it gets cold!"

Realizing his speculative gaze was still on her, Cara murmured something about setting another place and hurried on ahead of him. She busied herself getting out the silver, extra butter, and oyster crackers, and once they'd begun eating, the excellent chowder took the attention of both men.

But after his third bowl, Sheriff Ross eyed his elaborately nonchalant uncle—who acted as though it were the most natural thing in the world to have a pretty woman in his kitchen—and said, "Okay, Uncle Virgil, tell me how you managed to get Miss Morgan, actress, to cook your lunch?"

"Why, she comes three times a week and cooks my lunch, Dal." Then, as he realized exactly what Dal had said, he asked, "Actress? What do you mean, actress?"

"That's what she told me. You mean she told you something different?"

"She's the new Senior Services home visitor," Virgil

said, dabbing his mouth with a blue-checked napkin. "Cara, you never said anything being an actress. Been holding out on me?"

"I...not exactly, Virgil," she said, seeing the skeptical look on Dallas Ross's face. Why did it matter? Deciding it didn't, she got up and began clearing the table.

"Miss Morgan, are you or are you not the Senior Services home visitor?"

Dallas Ross's blunt question got under her skin. She gathered all the silver and put it into sudsy water. "I am."

"And are you an actress?"

"Yes, Sheriff, I am! Well, I've been in a lot of little theatre productions back home, and I intend to organize one here at the Senior Center."

"You do?" said Virgil, a sly grin on his face as he watched the two of them. "First I've heard of it."

"That's because I just thought of it," admitted Cara. Then as she realized the possibilities, she grew excited. "They do have a stage at the Center, and I know there are lots of people who'd be great on the boards."

"Not me," Virgil said grumpily.

"Oh, sure you would," said Cara. "Really you'd love it. It's exciting, and there's nothing quite like knowing the audience is with you, that they're out there, listening to every—"

"If you'll pardon me, I have work to do," interrupted Dal. "Uncle Virgil, I brought my tools and all the materials, so don't say a word. I'm going to fix that roof today."

"I told you I'd get to that, boy," he said, glowering in very much the same way Cara had seen the sheriff do.

She headed off any further objections. "Sheriff, there's also a broken window in the front, and I can show you a couple of new leaks in the roof. I think you should consider new insulation in the ceiling while you're at it."

27

"You do, hm? Well, just make me a list, and I'll take care of it."

"Right. I will." Cara seemed either immune to Dal's mild sarcasm or determined to ignore it. "Virgil, your medication is by your plate—don't forget it."

The men exchanged glances, but Virgil took his pills, and Dal picked up his tools and started out of the kitchen. At the door he paused and said, "By the way, I decided it was best to go ahead and install those locks, Miss Morgan."

"You *what?*"

"I installed the dead-bolt locks on your back and front doors."

"But, Sheriff Ross, I definitely told you I couldn't afford them now!"

"You can pay me later," he said, his tone firm.

Virgil must have sensed the situation was close to explosive. "Say, how about if you cook dinner for him? That should be a treat for him."

"But hardly adequate payment," objected Cara.

"Oh, I don't know about that," said Virgil, his eyes going from one to the other. "Tell you what, how about if I come, too, in case you need a referee and because I think you're a mighty fine cook. I haven't been out in quite a spell."

This last statement was a fine bit of blackmail, and Cara succumbed to it. "I suppose if you're coming, too…"

"It's all settled," said Virgil with satisfaction. "How's tomorrow night? And what are we having?"

"Yes, Miss Morgan," put in Sheriff Ross, "what are we having?"

Cara grinned and shrugged her shoulders. "Who knows? Right now, I've got to get to work, or I'll never make my next appointment. I'll leave your list on the table, Sheriff."

He nodded and went out without another word, obviously wondering just who had come out on top in the confrontation.

As soon as he left, Cara lit into Virgil. "Now, Virgil—"

"How did you two meet?"

"On the beach the other night and don't try to make anything out of it," she retorted as she plunged her hands vigorously into the dishwater. "He doesn't even like me."

"Sure, and I'm a monkey's uncle," Virgil said on his way out the door.

"Close, Virgil Penhollow, close!" said Cara, wondering about her feelings. They were new, sort of exciting and not a little disturbing. To calm them, she began planning the menu for tomorrow night's dinner. That was no easy task, for she'd have to confine herself mainly to what she had on hand. Oh, well, she was used to making something out of nothing, and she never shied away from a good challenge.

Cara had an idea that fixing dinner on a shoestring was nothing compared to getting along with Sheriff Dallas Ross. And in the back of her mind she kept wondering how Janet Moody got along with him and why she had gone so far away and if they... Cara pushed the thought of Janet Moody even farther back into the corner of her mind.

Chapter Three

Cara always tried to be as unobtrusive as possible while she worked at the Stewarts'. Both Tom and Mary were always saying she did entirely too much. Before her stroke, Mary had been a fine homemaker, and Tom had just never gotten the hang of the whole process. He tried hard, but somehow the infinite variety of tasks eluded him. So Cara said nothing about the dusty shelves and the eggy forks. She just worked a little harder and a little faster, all the while seeming to be puttering. It was quite an act, but she suspected that while Tom bought it, Mary was well aware of it.

Tom was helping Mary, who sat in her wheelchair, finish her breakfast, and as always, Cara was in awe of Tom's infinite care and patience. Never a hint of anything but love and concern showed in his earnest face.

"There, darlin', you've done really well today!" he said as she finished the last of the omelet he was so justly proud of. Tom's once light brown hair was almost all gray now and carefully parted and combed to show the slight, but attractive wave in it. His eyes were blue, and he usually wore a blue shirt or sweater that made them look even bluer. Cara thought she'd never seen a man with a sweeter smile.

Mary chewed carefully and swallowed, something she had been unable to do well for quite a while, then said slowly, "Tom, you—it was very good." Her speech had improved greatly since Cara had started coming to help, but she was still often frustrated in her attempts to translate her thoughts into the right words.

With the dusting almost done, Cara decided to tackle the bookshelf, which also held photographs and various memorabilia. The Stewarts lived in a compact mobile home, nice and fairly new, and everything had its place. A wedding photograph of the couple caught her attention. "Oh!" she exclaimed, polishing its surface, "this is a beautiful picture." Tom Stewart, so tall and good-looking in his white Navy uniform, was looking down adoringly at Mary, who wore a creamy white lace dress. Its high, pointed collar kissed each side of Mary's gentle jaw, and the long sleeves fit tightly to her wrists. "You were a spectacular bride, Mrs. Stewart."

For a moment Cara thought that perhaps she'd said the wrong thing. But the stricken look that flashed across Mary Stewart's face—with its slightly drooping left side—was replaced with a crooked little smile. She was still a very pretty woman, with her pink complexion and silvery blond hair. Her eyes were blue, like her husband's, and she looked up at him. "We did have a wonderful wedding."

Tom stacked the dishes, his eyes on his wife. "That's not what Cara said, darlin'. She said you were a spectacular bride, and that's the gospel truth. Fair took my breath away, you did, when you walked down the aisle toward me—"

Mary made a pained sound in her throat. "Can't walk now."

"But you will, darlin'. You will."

As Tom carried the dishes into the kitchen, Cara thought of the quiet determination with which he tackled every phase of Mary's rehabilitation. "Did someone make your dress?" she asked softly. The relationship between Mary and Tom Stewart was not always comfortable for her. Mary's underlying belief that she no longer deserved Tom's devotion because of her helplessness bothered Cara more than she'd admitted to anyone. "I've always thought I'd like to be married in a dress like that."

"Would you like to see it?" Each word seemed an effort, but Mary got them out, and there was a look of pleasure on her face that wasn't there often.

"I'd love to!"

At the sound of her delighted exclamation, Tom came in from the kitchen, wiping his hands on a dish towel. "What's all the excitement about?"

"My wedding…" The word had left her, and Mary got that frustrated look again. Though it was difficult, neither Tom nor Cara made a move to supply the word, because that would further humiliate Mary. Finally, her face twisted with the effort, she said, "gown."

Relieved, Cara felt she could now say, "Mary said I could see her wedding dress, Tom."

He nodded, carefully masking his pain at Mary's little lapse. "I think I saw it when we cleaned the cupboards last spring. Top shelf in the bedroom?" Mary nodded and he went to get it.

When he brought it out, Cara was enchanted. She held it up and twirled around a time or two. "I'll bet I'm not too fat for it!"

Tom smiled. "You're old enough to be thinking of your own dress, your own wedding."

Once again the face of Sheriff Dallas Ross flashed into her mind. "Oh, I've got lots of time, and besides, who'd have a noodlehead like me?"

"Any man with…with half a brain like me!" said Mary, her smile real and lovely.

Tom laughed. This was the Mary he knew. "Mary, darlin', you were the prettiest thing God ever made, in that dress."

"How long have you two been married, anyway?" asked Cara.

"It will be fifty years in December," Tom said quietly,

his eyes on Mary as though he saw her as a bride, the way she'd been before the stroke.

"*Fifty years?*" asked Cara incredulously. "That's neat!"

"Neat," Mary said, her eyes meeting Tom's for a moment, then veering away.

As though he'd read her thoughts, Tom said, "We always planned to renew our vows, do it all over again, on our fiftieth anniversary."

"I think that's a wonderful idea," enthused Cara.

But Mary shook her head. "I want to walk to you the same."

"You will," said Tom quietly, stubbornly, but Mary only shook her head again.

Cara spoke without thinking, in her need to banish the uncomfortable tension. "Say, I just had an idea. Wouldn't it be great if we asked around and got some other wedding dresses and lots of other clothes, too, and had an old-time style show? The ones who still fit in them could wear their own, and the others with more...ah, mature figures could let somebody model them. What do you think?" Her brown eyes were snapping now at the idea, though she'd only brought it up impulsively.

"Sounds good to me," said Tom, relieved that the awkward moment had passed. "Now my Mary could still fit into hers, but—" Realizing he might have said exactly the wrong thing, he hastened to add, "But I'll bet she wouldn't mind if you modeled it, Cara. Looks like you two are about the same size. What do you say, Mary?" Anxiously he watched her face.

In a tremulous voice she replied, "I say both of you...have good ideas."

"I'd be honored to wear your dress, Mary, and I promise to be very careful with it." Cara looked squarely into the older woman's eyes. "Then you can wear it in December for your anniversary celebration."

Tom cleared his throat. "Well, you know what they

say, 'a woman's work is never done.' That's true for sure when a man's doing it. I'll leave you two to your woman talk." His gaze rested on his wife for a long moment. Then he turned and went back to the kitchen.

It was a while before Cara, as she finished her dusting, gathered the courage to venture, "Tom is really a fine man, isn't he? I hope I find one like him."

Mary's nod was slow. To Cara's chagrin the woman's eyes filled with tears. "Better than I deserve."

"That's not so, Mary! He loves you, and everything he does is because of that. Surely you know—"

"I know he spends his days waiting on me, and I can't be…or do…or give…." She stifled a little sob. "I'm useless, not…not even pretty anymore."

"That's not true, not any of it." Cara wanted desperately to say more, to offer words of comfort, but could think of nothing. Feeling helpless, she carefully folded the dress, put it on the sofa, then put the picture which had started the whole thing back on the bookshelf. As she did, she saw something she hadn't seen before, a vibrantly colored seed catalogue. "Is this your catalogue?"

Mary glanced over apathetically, then nodded.

"Who's the gardener?—you, or Tom?"

"We both were…before."

Cara winced. Such flat, final words. A vague plan emerging in her mind, she asked, "Mind if I take it with me? I might want to order some seeds." Another nod was all she got. Mary's eyes were closed now. Cara placed the catalogue beside her purse and resumed her duties without any further conversation, but her mind was going a mile a minute.

Cara spent an average of two hours at each client's house, and most of the time seemed to speed by. Not so with Ladell Abernethy, who lived next door to the Stewarts. Although Miss Abernethy at sixty-eight was younger than many of Cara's other people, she somehow seemed older. Not even Cara was successful in her efforts to keep Miss Abernethy's spirits up. She even suspected that the woman found a perverse pleasure in finding the dark side of every situation.

Cara chided herself for that little judgment as she parted the curtains in the tiny living room. Miss Abernethy, seated in her usual place in front of the television set, put up a hand to her eyes.

"Oh, Miss Morgan, it's so bright!"

"Yes, isn't it wonderful? We've got sunshine today, the first time this week." Hoping the sun would cheer Miss Abernethy up in spite of herself, Cara stood looking out the window, enjoying the lovely afternoon. No ocean view here, but she could see a couple of free-wheeling gulls in the cloudless blue sky. For a moment she wished that she were as free as they looked. But only for a moment.

She stifled the thought that Miss Abernethy had moaned all week because the weather was so dull, so gray. "How do you feel today?" It was a careful, dutiful question, asked because she knew the woman wanted to tell her.

"My back is really bothering me," she said with what Cara felt was indecently close to satisfaction. "We might have to call Dr. Zylius again."

Cara hid her smile. She strongly suspected that Miss Abernethy harbored feelings very close to an adolescent crush on the town's new bachelor doctor. That he was nearer Cara's age than Miss Abernethy's didn't seem to matter. "Have you been doing those exercises he prescribed?"

Miss Abernethy laid her head back and sighed, "No, I'm not at all sure they're right for me."

"They're right," Cara said firmly. "Would you like for me to do them with you? I used to with my grandma."

"Certainly not! If I did them at all, it would have to be in total privacy. Really, Miss Morgan, you don't always use good judgment." She glared at Cara, her expression haughty, then closed her eyes with another sigh.

Cara merely nodded and busied herself straightening up the piles of newspapers and magazines that seemed to multiply like flies. She only came to Miss Abernethy's for an hour, three times a week, and she had to admit that was enough. No matter how hard she tried, the woman found something wrong with every plan she devised. When she had everything stacked neatly she said, "I'll tie these papers up and take them over to the fire station. The Boy Scouts are having a paper drive, and—"

"You'll do no such thing! Put them on the back porch with the others."

"But, Miss Abernethy, the porch is jammed already," Cara said, trying to keep her voice steady. She couldn't deny that the woman bothered her. Her own attitude wasn't much better than Miss Abernethy's. She knew it, and couldn't seem to help it.

"Then stack them more efficiently. You are rather haphazard in your approach, Miss Morgan. Oh, I've watched you whizzing along and singing, and…" She paused, then added slowly, "slopping through your work. I've seriously considered complaining to your supervisor."

"Oh, please don't do that!" Cara was painfully aware that she couldn't afford to lose the hours here. "I do try—"

"Trying isn't always enough. You don't really consider my feelings. You try to push me into things beyond my ability."

"I'm sorry." Cara's tone was quiet, her eyes downcast. But she honestly believed that her suggestions were right for the woman. "I'll finish straightening up and fix something for your dinner. What would you like?"

"Anything but another Italian dish," she said with a thin smile. Cara had surprised her with lasagne she'd brought from home a couple of weeks ago. Since then, not a visit had gone by without a comment about how it just wasn't the thing for a woman with her delicate di-

37

gestion—although she'd eaten every bit of it.

"Um…anything?" Cara knew better than that. There was a long list of things that Miss Abernethy couldn't— or wouldn't—tolerate. Realizing that she might strike out again, Cara timidly ventured, "Do you like potato soup?"

A thoughtful, almost pensive expression crossed the old woman's face. "My mother used to make potato soup."

Thinking she'd hit on something, Cara said, "I'll start some."

"Of course, you'll have to leave out the onions and celery, and don't put much salt, and no pepper. My digestion is delicate, you know."

"No pepper, celery, or onions," echoed Cara. She sighed, knowing that Dr. Zylius had said that Miss Abernethy could eat anything at all. Before Miss Abernethy had a chance to tell her, Cara said, "I'll make absolutely sure I leave the kitchen spotless. Really I will."

Feeling cheated out of warning Cara, Miss Abernethy said, "See that you do. I found a spot on the wall behind the stove the last time you were here. You're always zipping around." Her eyes narrowed. "Why, I could get someone who would work half as fast as you do, for only three dollars an hour, too."

"But Miss Abernethy, you don't—" Cara stopped short of saying, *You don't pay me anything….* Not knowing whether she wanted to giggle at the ridiculous statement or bawl, all she allowed herself to say was, "Yes, ma'am."

"And before you leave the room, pull that shade down." Miss Abernethy put a hand over her eyes, as if to emphasize the fact that it did, indeed, hurt them terribly.

Cara did as she was bidden without further comment. As she fixed the unappetizing meal in Miss Abernethy's dim little kitchen, she felt like a colossal failure, and low in general. Then she remembered that Virgil and Sheriff Ross were coming to dinner, and her natural good spirits reasserted themselves.

Let's see... she mused, *the chicken will go far enough if I make noodles, and I have those home-canned green beans that Mom sent back the last time I went home, and for dessert...*

"Miss Morgan! I've called three times. *What* are you *doing* in there?" The imperious tone grated on Cara's nerves, but she summoned a smile and hurried in to see what she'd done wrong now. It was going to be a long, long hour.

That evening as he knocked on the door of Rose Cottage, Dal Ross glanced down and checked his clothes. Beneath the dark tweed jacket, he wore a brown crewneck sweater over a blue shirt, with its button-down collar neatly tucked, and his tan cords were well broken in. Hoping he wasn't dressed too casually, he wondered what the theatrical Miss Morgan would be wearing. She opened the door just then and stared at him until he said, "May I come in?"

"But Mr. Penhollow isn't with you!"

One dark brow raised, Dallas said, "Am I to understand that since my uncle was unable to come, I'm not welcome?"

"I...it's just that I thought he was coming," murmured Cara.

Another little silence passed, during which he stood quietly, still watching her. "Maybe it would be better if I don't stay after all. I can see that you'd rather I didn't."

As he turned to go, Cara took a step and caught his arm. "Oh, don't go. I didn't mean you weren't welcome. In fact, I want...I'd like very much for you to stay. Unless, of course, you'd rather not."

There was a dim light burning above their heads and his glance roved over the exceedingly feminine outfit she wore. A cream-colored lacy blouse came right up to

39

her chin, with a cameo pinned at the throat, and her brown skirt was very long and full. He didn't know much about fabrics, but it looked as though it were soft, maybe velvet, and once again he got the impression that she'd stepped out of an old photograph. But his next comment wasn't about her clothing. "I suppose a bachelor can't afford to miss a home-cooked meal. Is that chicken I smell?"

"Yes. Oh, I hope it isn't burned!" Realizing simultaneously that she still held tightly to his arm and that the chicken had been done fifteen minutes ago, Cara let go, spun around, and flew to the kitchen, leaving him standing there. After a moment he shook his head, stepped inside, and shut the door behind him.

The room was as pleasant and inviting as he remembered. Sheriff Dallas Ross had done a great deal of thinking about the two encounters he'd had with Cara Morgan, and it had taken every persuasive power his uncle possessed to induce him to come here alone tonight. However, Virgil's excuse that he wasn't feeling well had rung uncomfortably true. Dal was worried about the old man.

He looked around, took in the lace-covered little table, set with candles, no less, in front of the fire. The soft sound of romantic music made him feel uneasy. He sat in the comfortable red plush chair with the strange conviction that he ought to resist the whole thing, especially Miss Cara-Honey Morgan.

But when she came back in, her face flushed and rosy, the chicken borne triumphantly up in the air, he couldn't keep from smiling at her. "That smells good."

"It is. My mom's a good cook, and she's been trying to teach me for years."

Later, as he ate the last of his ginger apricot creme, Dal said, "Miss Morgan, your mother did a good job teaching you to cook. You can tell her I said so."

Her eyes shining with pleasure, Cara said, "Thanks, I will. I'm going over to visit my folks in a couple of weeks." The main topic of dinner conversation had been about how he had chosen law-enforcement as a career, and he had to admit Cara was a good listener. She sat with her chin resting on both palms, elbows on the table.

"And you—" Dal stopped. He'd been about to say how very pretty she looked in the candlelight. That made him stop and wonder. He was not a man given to extravagant compliments or to talking about himself.

Cara leaned forward a little, her mobile mouth curved into a smile, her dark brown eyes intent. "What were you going to say?"

Gruffly he answered, "That you're falling down on your job as a hostess." She looked so crestfallen that before she could ask what he meant, he said, "The music stopped five minutes ago, and you didn't put another record on. Isn't that all part of this scene you set?"

A tiny look of hurt flitted across her face, but she covered it well as she got up and efficiently stacked the few remaining dishes. "I'll see to it. And we're even now, Sheriff." It was his turn to look perplexed, and as she paused at the door, her expression was mischievous. "You said *I* made fun of *you* the other day."

Thinking she couldn't have been farther from the truth, he watched her come back into the room, after taking her time choosing an album. When he heard the lovely, lilting strains of Strauss, he said, "I might have known you'd like waltzes."

With a graceful little shrug she came over to him, her feet lightly moving 1-2-3 in time to "Tales from the Vienna Woods." "Lady's choice. Sir, may I have the pleasure of this waltz?" Her eyes were laughing, her mouth was laughing, and he couldn't resist, although something in him warned that he should at least try.

"I haven't danced since I was in high school," he protested. She caught his hands and pulled him to his feet, and he noticed that all her nails were bitten close.

"Come on, before it's over!"

He found himself with one hand clasped tightly in hers, the other placed on her slim waist. She felt so lithe and soft at the same time. The music wasn't loud, but it filled the room, filled his head as they made swirling, soft circles around the crowded front room. Their bodies were not touching, but the fragrance of her, of her hair, reached his senses. A faint hint of roses, of...of lemon...

Suddenly he tripped, and both of them tumbled and ended in a heap on the carpet. Fleetingly he thought again of how soft she was for someone so slender, and he found that her breathless laughing face was very near his own. Her eyes were shut, and he was so tempted to kiss her that he pushed her away instead. "I'm sorry," he said abruptly.

"For what?" She gave him an unreadable look as she pulled herself up, then extended a hand. "Unless you tripped me on purpose!"

He managed to get to his feet without her help. "Of course I didn't do it on purpose. Are you all right?" She nodded, that look still in her eyes, still too close for him to be comfortable. "I should be going."

"Oh, it's early. I promise to behave. Really I will." She was smiling again. "I know, let's play Scrabble."

But he shook his head. "No, I'd better go. Thanks for dinner."

"We'll do it again, closer to payday."

"Miss Morgan, I'm not sure that would be a good idea." The look on her face now made him wish he could take back the words.

"I see." Her chin lifted, and she managed to keep her smile intact. "I think I understand. You were manipulated into coming over here by your uncle, and I embarrassed you by asking you to dance, and besides, I'm probably not the kind of woman you care to be with!"

The rush of words was too uncomfortably close to the truth for him to deny. "Look, don't take it personally—"

"Oh, can it, Sheriff! That's what people always say just after they've said something unbearably personal. Don't worry. I wouldn't go out with you if for some awful reason you had to ask me."

He looked as if he might want to say something further; instead he nodded and turned to go. As she brushed past him on her way to open the door, he caught that hint of roses again and steeled himself against it. "Good night, Miss Morgan."

Cara smiled the whole eternity it seemed to take for him to cross the room and go past her into the darkness. Then she shut the door firmly behind him. With a croaky little sob, she put her back to it.

"What a mess you made of that, Cara!" The breathy sound of her words was lost in the sudden stillness. The waltz was over, the dinner was over, the whole thing was over. "I don't care...I don't care!"

But she did care, very much. As she moped about, straightening up, all she could think of was those few brief moments when they'd fallen, how she'd felt when he seemed about to kiss her.

"Forget it, Cara. He's not for you. Or more to the point, you're not for him." She would have given in to tears then, but she heard the plaintive meow of the cat that had adopted her a week or so before. When she opened the door the green-eyed yellow tabby she'd named Miss Scarlett stood there, her expression clearly readable: *Any chicken left for me?* Cara laughed and caught the furry creature up in her arms, then closed the door and carefully turned the sturdy new dead-bolt lock.

Chapter Four

Not only was Cara unable to forget the evening with Dal Ross, but it plagued her thoughts all the next week. She went about her work, perhaps accomplished even more than she ordinarily did, which was plenty. Besides her duties with Seretha—who was far from well—Tom and Mary, Ladell Abernethy, and Virgil Penhollow, whose curiosity about her and his nephew was obvious and enormous, she was able to get the style show all set up for Saturday evening. It hadn't been an easy task, but she'd welcomed the extra work. Being busy during the day and tired at night helped to take her mind off Tillicum's finest.

However, on Saturday afternoon Cara discovered she had some spare time. Everything was set for the style show that evening, and she'd even made herself balance her checkbook, as near to balanced as it ever got. The facts were inescapable. The little cottage was definitely beyond her budget. With a sigh, she went for her coat and hat. Walking on the beach made everything more bearable, from not having enough money, to…not being the kind of woman the sheriff wanted to take out.

There was a light drizzle, and the sun was hiding behind a soft, dove-colored sky. But as Cara strode along the sand, her spirits lifted, and she found herself talking to God as she often did on the beach. Somehow the endless expanse of sky, the awesome power and sound of the ocean, brought her thoughts to Him.

Lord, I'm so glad to be able to walk here like this, to have meaningful work that's good and right for me. The little shore birds...*Are they sandpipers?*...interrupted their smorgasbord choosing and flew as she neared, but not far away. It seemed to Cara that they were willing to share the beach with her, from a respectable distance, at least. "And God," she whispered, "thanks for birds! And rain..."

Lifting her face to the cold, gently falling mist, she breathed deeply of the incredibly fresh air. *Lord, I do praise you! If only I could please you just a tiny fraction as much as you do me.* She started walking again, and the face of Dal Ross came into her mind. He possessed traits she admired in a man—strong, settled in his life, happy in his work, he loved the ocean...and he was so good-looking. Common sense told her that part of her opinion was the old "beauty in the eye of the beholder" bit, that the way she felt about him affected how handsome she thought he was.

The truth is, Cara, a man like Dal Ross would never fall for a girl like you. Just think how he reacted the other night. He had a chance to make a move, and he ran like a scalded dog! Thinking of the disastrous end to the evening with Dal and of her neat little house that she'd have to leave the first of November made her suddenly start to jog down the beach. She soon came to the huge outcropping of stone known as Cape Perpetua. There was no way to get around it, especially this late in the year. In fact, she'd run out of sandy beach and come to a stretch of rocky terrain that was pretty forbidding. Her attention was caught by a ravine cut far into the rocky shore. Its little waterfall looked so inviting, she made up her mind to try to get to it.

There was a trail of sorts etched faintly into the side of the grassy slope, and if she didn't stop to look down as the ocean flung and foamed itself farther and farther along the sandy floor thirty feet below her, Cara did fine. The tide was coming in. She was about to turn around when suddenly, the rain-soaked trail dropped away beneath her right foot, instinctively causing her to fall forward onto the wet earth to her left.

Heart racing, chest tight, she lay still for a moment, very much aware now of the pounding of the surf below as it clawed its way to the back of the ravine. When her breathing and her heart slowed, she'd definitely made up her mind to turn back. But when she straightened and looked down, she saw that more than half of the already narrow trail had clattered down the rocky incline. There was a space of perhaps eight inches left, scant room for only one of her feet. She would either have to crawfish or flatten herself against the hillside and inch her way along the broken trail.

"You can do it, Cara...." She repeated the words a couple of times, then drew in her breath sharply, knowing that she could not, after all, force herself to go back the way she'd come. Though the rain was falling in earnest now, at least the wind was minimal. But the relentless water below was now well beyond the precarious place where she stood and was close to joining the waterfall's pool at the foot of the cleft in the rock. So she went forward with a confidence that was mostly sheer grit.

It took about fifteen minutes for her to skirt the tiny trail and duck behind the graceful fall of water for a brief respite. She gazed out in awe at the boiling, stormy waters of the Pacific Ocean. Then she found herself on the other side, where, perversely, the trail was wide and easy. Now the Cape itself was the obstacle at the end of the nice trail. Wet to the skin, Cara sat on a fairly flat rock to assess her situation.

After a few moments, she saw that she had two options. One was to return the way she'd come; the other was to climb straight up the vegetation-covered cliff, to the highway two hundred feet above her on the left. Something deep within her made Cara realize she couldn't retrace her steps. Just the memory of that one-shoe-width trail made her stomach knot again. After digesting that little bit of self-knowledge, she sat quietly in the rain for perhaps ten minutes, willing herself to enjoy the dazzling, spectacular view. She prepared her body for the climb and asked God to be with her. At least the incline looked fairly gradual.

About a third of the way up, Cara was once more breathing heavily. It was not at all gradual; it was *steep*. Each time she thought she had a foothold it slithered from beneath her, and it seemed at times that for every step she took she slid back two, on her muddy front. The days of rain had loosened roots and rotted the spongy earth mass to a treacherous depth. Cara wasn't afraid of slugs or bugs or spiders, which was a good thing, for she encountered more than one of each face to face. She began chanting the few names she knew of the plants that offered a hand and then, more often than not, broke in her grasp.

"Salal, scotch broom, salmon berries, blackberries..." Cara winced as the blackberry thorns, though mercifully soggy, tore at her palms. She'd made it half way to the top when an awful thought hit her. *Poison ivy.* If there was any around, she would get it. Her poison ivy allergy was violent and had once put her in the hospital.

"Oh, dear Father, *please* don't let there be any poison ivy! Please?" She rarely asked such things in her

48

prayers, but she asked it now. Every so often she repeated the little plea as she clawed her weary way to the top, which seemed to be farther away at times instead of nearer. A few minutes short of an hour later she heaved herself the last few feet of the way and collapsed in a little heap.

A hand on her shoulder, and a familiar voice made her stomach sink back almost to where she'd climbed from. It couldn't be, but it was. Sheriff Dallas Ross himself.

"Miss Morgan, are you all right?"

Cara hauled her body to her feet, determined to stand up, look him right in the eye, and not even acknowledge the fact that she looked like the wreck of the Hesperus. "Of course I'm all right, Sheriff. Can't you think of any other opening lines? I was just taking a little hike—" The fib slipped from her lips just as her knees buckled.

He caught her before she fell. His arms were warm and tight around her. "Here, let me help you to the car."

Too tired, too weak to protest, she leaned against him as he slowly walked her over to his car. She had to admit, she'd never been handled with more tenderness. "What are you doing here? How did you know I—"

"The man who lives on the bluff called the office and said some crazy girl was trying to conquer the cape." He helped her into the front seat, shrugging off her protests that she was wet and muddy. Then he went around to get into the driver's seat. "That was quite a climb. I wasn't sure you'd make those last few feet."

Cara's eyes, closed in weariness, flew open. "You've been watching me?" At his grave nod, she said, "How long, and why didn't you help me?"

He shrugged again at her angry tone. "Even if you'd fallen you couldn't have fallen far, with all that underbrush. I couldn't see how I could help you, and you weren't in any danger, so I just—"

"You just watched. You thought, 'the crazy girl got herself into this mess, and it'll do her good to get herself out.' "

"You've got to admit it was a dumb stunt. What made you decide to go around Dead Man's Inlet, anyway?"

"Dead Man's Inlet?"

"That's what some of the natives have called it ever since a man's body washed up into there. One of my more intriguing cases."

"Really." Cara tried without success to keep her teeth from chattering. "If you wouldn't mind taking me home, I'd appreciate it, Sheriff Ross."

He nodded and started the engine, turning the heater on full blast, for Cara had begun to shiver violently.

She didn't speak again during the short ride to her cottage. When he braked in front she started to get out, but he reached over to detain her. "Look, I'm sorry if you felt I wasn't helpful enough. Forgive me." His tone was…almost humble.

"Of course." She tried to pull away, but he held her fast. "I need to go in, Sheriff Ross. Let me go—"

"Not until you know how glad I am you're all right."

"I'm *not* all right!" she burst out, the scalding tears overflowing. "I'm freezing to death and soaked to the skin and dirty and scratched and embarrassed right up to my eyeballs!"

He slid across the seat, reached over and opened the door, then gently urged her out. His arm was around her as they made their way down the path, her feet stumbling, his sure and steady. As he reached the threshold he said very quietly, "Your key, do you have it with you?"

Stricken, she nonetheless decided to brazen it out. "I was only going to be gone for a little while, so it's not locked."

He surprised her. With no recriminations, no lectures, he guided her in and gave orders for her to shed her wet clothes and take a hot bath. When she stood trembling in the middle of the living room, he gave her a slight push. "Go on and do what I told you. I'll heat some cider."

"There...there isn't any...."

"Then I'll make some tea. Go on."

She obeyed him then and was grateful beyond words as she slipped into a rose-fragrant tub of hot water. Twenty minutes later she came out, wrapped in a long black velvet robe. A gift from one of her more affluent friends, it made her look quite elegant, except that her hair was damp and tousled and her feet were bare. Gratefully she took the mug of hot, sweet tea. "Thank you."

"Sit down here by the fire," Dal urged, his hand at her back, propelling her to the blue chair. He'd built a fine, snapping fire, and it was irresistible even though she'd stopped shivering.

"Thank you," she said again, faintly this time, as she sat down. "Why are you being so nice?" She put one slender foot on top of the other. "My feet are still cold."

He sat on the floor and took her feet in his hands, which were very warm. Somehow, Cara found that she couldn't speak. It seemed an almost unbearably intimate thing for him to hold her feet in his hands. He didn't look up for a long time. When he did, he found himself gazing straight into her wide, brown, questioning eyes. "You must not have a very high opinion of me."

"Why?" she asked, almost in a whisper.

"If you ask a man why he's acting nice, it must mean you think he's not, most of the time." He was slowly, gently massaging her feet as he spoke.

Cara fleetingly thought how grateful she was that she

was vain about her feet and took such good care of them. It was partly because she was fastidious about her whole body and partly because she had very pretty feet. They were narrow and had well-shaped toes, with nails polished a pale pink. Not her fingernails, just her toenails. Her fingernails were always a disaster. Aloud all she said was, "I...I think you're..." She faltered, no more able to put into words the sudden surge of feeling for the man literally at her feet than she could take wings and fly. Instead she blurted, "Why did your folks name you Dallas?"

He looked a little startled, but he said, "Um, because I was born in Dallas, Texas, I think. My dad was in the service."

She giggled. "Good thing you weren't born in Waxahatchie!" He couldn't keep from from grinning, too, at the thought, but before he could reply, Cara asked, "What time is it?"

He glanced at his watch. "Five-thirty. Why?"

She jumped up suddenly, narrowly avoiding stomping his hands. "I've got to be at the Senior Center at six, to handle all of the last minute details—"

"Get ready. I'll take care of the fire and drive you over."

"You don't have to," she said at the door to her bedroom.

"Oh, yes, I do."

She didn't ask why. "Thank you. I'll only be a minute."

"I've heard *that* before," he said wryly, as he poked at the fire.

"I'll just bet you have, and from more women than I could shake a stick at," muttered Cara as she swung the door shut and flew to her closet.

The outfit Cara chose was one of her favorites, although she knew from his lightly startled look that, once again, Sheriff Ross didn't approve. She slipped into her fur jacket and they left.

He affirmed her suspicions as he pulled out onto the highway and headed toward town. "May I ask a question?"

"You want to know if I'm wearing a nightgown, right?"

His face told her that she was correct, even before he said, "I thought so when I first saw you come out, and I told myself that not even you would go out in your nightgown."

Cara sighed a little. She should have thought of what his reaction would be before she put it on. She looked down. The soft white muslin Victorian nightgown was opaque. It had a high collar that hugged her neck, sleeves that drooped lace past her wrists, and lace on the bottom that flirted with her ankles. It also had quite possibly eight voluminous yards of fabric in it, which she'd belted tightly with a forget-me-not blue sash wrapped around her waist several times and tucked in. "Sheriff Ross, nothing but my face, hands and feet show, isn't that so?" He glanced over at her in the gloom and nodded, not speaking as his eyes swept from her now fluffy halo of gold-brown hair to the tips of her flat, ballet-style slippers. "And you couldn't see through it back at the house, right?"

"Miss Morgan!" he said, sounding slightly shocked.

"Well, you can't," she said defiantly. "I know, because I'm wearing a full-length petticoat underneath."

"Maybe so, but it's still not…it's just not proper," he insisted stubbornly.

"Impropriety is in the eye of the beholder," paraphrased Cara in a discreet murmur. A little more loudly and with the feeling she was doing herself out of an escort for the evening, she said, "You can just let me out at the back door of the Senior Center. I can see how a man like you wouldn't want to be seen in public with a woman in her nightgown."

The cool words fell into an uneasy silence, and it was a mile or so before he said unwillingly, "Actually, it looks very…um…pretty on you."

"Thank you."

He waited for her to say more and must have realized she wasn't going to make it easy for him. "I did sort of promise Virgil I'd be there."

"He's coming?" Cara's coolness melted away. "Oh, I hope so! The old rascal, he needs to get out more."

"You two seem to get along very well."

"Virgil accepts me just as I am."

Dal didn't reply to the pointed statement, but as he drove near the converted church and its assorted annexes that comprised the Center, he said, "I'll let you out and park in the back and—"

"So you won't have to walk in with me?"

"Look, Miss Morgan, I—"

"Thanks for the ride, Sheriff." She had the car door open almost before he'd come to a complete stop and was out before he could finish his sentence. He sat there for a moment, watching her run inside, left with only the faint fragrance of lemon and roses.

An hour later Sheriff Ross, who had stood in the back of the darkened room through the entire show, watched with a full house as Cara, the last model, walked slowly out onto the stage, turned with what looked like professional skill, and gave a lovely view of the full train that flowed from Mary Stewart's wedding dress.

The whole style show had been a rousing success. There'd been flappers in knee-length, beaded creations, their smiles outdoing their sags and wrinkles; tidy thirties dresses; and some wide-shouldered, severely tailored, Joan Crawfordish outfits from the forties. Because of Cara's cajoling many of the women had modeled their own clothes or vintage clothing Cara had managed to find.

But it was Cara, in the ivory lace dress, who stole the show. As she turned around to face the audience again, her smile as radiant as a real bride's, she heard one of the men call out, "Sing for us, Cara!" She shook her head, but Mrs. Johnson had already begun an introduction. "Sing, Cara, sing!" There were even some footstompers joining in now, and the call was taken up all over the room. *"Sing!"*

Cara strained to see. There were no real spotlights, but there were some fairly bright lights above the stage and to each side. She had looked for Dal Ross, but hadn't seen him come in, nor did she see him anywhere in the audience now. He must have taken her seriously and left, and it was just as well.

She had sung several songs during their practice sessions during the week, and as Mrs. Johnson played a bit louder Cara recognized the tune. She nodded her head slightly and smiled...and began to sing, her low, husky voice soft at first, then gathering strength.

"Some day he'll come along, the man I love,
And he'll be big and strong, the man I love...."

She was enjoying herself enormously, knowing full well that everyone else was enjoying it, too. And when she sang, her voice full of feeling, "And so all else above, I'm waiting for...*the man I love,*" there was a wild, gratifying rush of applause, even some shouts of "Encore! Encore!" She just smiled and bowed as gracefully as she could within the confines of the sweeping dress, then turned to walk off the stage.

She did fine until she reached the stairs, where in her haste she turned her foot and found herself in a giggling heap. When she looked up and saw—who else—Sheriff Dallas Ross nearby, she choked out, "Don't ask if I'm all right. I am. I am!" He took her elbow and lifted her up, and she saw Virgil standing just behind him, his face bright and interested.

"That was tip-top, girl! You sing almost as good as you make chowder," Virgil said to Cara, but his eyes were on Dal's face.

"Yes, Miss Morgan," murmured Dal, "you constantly surprise me—"

He was interrupted as several of the others came up then, among them Tom Stewart, who was pushing Mary in her wheelchair. Mary's face was relaxed and happy-looking as she said, "That dress looks better on you than it ever did on me, Cara."

"I wouldn't say that," put in Tom gallantly. "And when you wear it for our anniversary celebration, everybody will see how fine you still look."

Mary's smile faded, and Cara bent down and hugged her. "He's right, you know. You mustn't give up. Tom is worth whatever it takes. Right?" Some instinct prompted the words, though she knew she might be putting more pressure on Mary than she should.

Dal had moved over to the side of the room and was watching Cara as she pushed Mary's wheelchair over to the gaily decorated refreshment table at the rear of the room. He saw Cara spread her hands over the fine lace of the dress, laugh, and say something. Cara Morgan seemed to laugh a lot. She was still laughing when she disappeared through a door at the side of the small stage. It gave him some time to think about the afternoon and evening, how he felt about them and Cara Morgan. She certainly wasn't like Janet in any way. She didn't always show good judgment—that escapade in Dead Man's Inlet could have ended quite differently. She seemed to have no friends but people who were twice or three times her age…and the same could be said for her clothes.

He shook his head as she reappeared, the white nightgown again belted tightly around her slender waist. She did look pretty in it, he admitted to himself. Then he quickly banished a stray vision of her beside a bed, the gown falling loose at her bare feet.

She has pretty feet, even if she does chew her fingernails, he thought. *And with encouragement, she could break that habit. She's kind and compassionate to older people, she likes dogs, and she laughs a lot.* The list wasn't bad. As she came closer he had just enough time to think that with a firm guiding hand she could outgrow some of those immature, aggravating habits. And after all, she certainly wasn't the kind of girl you'd want to marry. He'd already buried the picture of her in Mary's dress deep in his mind. He commanded himself to forget the sound of her husky voice singing, "I'm waiting for the man I love…."

"Did you enjoy the style show, Sheriff?" Cara asked as she came close enough.

"Very much, and so did everyone else. You must have a talent for arranging this kind of thing."

She smiled brightly at him. "Yes, I guess I do."

Not very modest, he added to the negative list. Yes, there was quite a bit he could do to help Cara Morgan grow up. He told himself that was the reason he asked, "Would you like to go out for coffee after you're through here?"

She looked at him keenly, then shook her head. "I don't think so. I…I'm really getting sort of stiff. That climbing business was, as you pointed out this afternoon, a dumb stunt, and I think I'm going to pay dearly for it in sore muscles."

"Are you about through here?" At her nod he said, "I'll take you home when you're ready."

"That won't be necessary." Her smile was sweet, polite, and a bit distant.

"I brought you, and I'll take you home."

She met his eyes for a long moment. Then she said slowly, "All right. Just let me make sure all the clothes we used are taken care of." She turned to go and cast one more slightly questioning glance at him.

As she mingled easily with the people, administering a warm hug here, a stroke there, Dallas Ross's gaze followed her, his expression thoughtful.

At her door almost an hour later, she took out her key with a grin. "See, Sheriff Ross, what you've done for me? I'm approaching the ranks of responsibility. I must thank you, kind sir!" She stood on tiptoe, obviously intending to kiss his cheek.

But he turned his head and leaned down slightly. Her lips were as smooth and sweet as they looked, and the kiss was no short, chaste, first-time kiss after all.

When she pulled away, breathless, a wondering look on her face, she said, "I—think maybe after that...you could call me Honey and I could call you Dal...."

He took the key from her, opened the door, shoved her gently inside, and returned the key. "Lock the door behind you." Then he walked quickly away. Cara did as he said. She closed the door and locked it before she walked to her bedroom as though she were already asleep.

Chapter Five

During her first hour at Seretha Hodges' the next day, Cara kept going in every so often to check on her, but all the older woman wanted to talk about was Dal.

"I feel fine, I tell you." The sound of her breathing didn't match the conviction of her words by any means. "Now tell me again what happened. Oh, I wish I'd been able to go! You wore Mary's wedding dress and sang 'The Man I Love,' and you thought he wasn't there, but he was. Now, what exactly did he say?"

Cara repeated what she remembered of the evening, except what had happened at her door. She'd been kissed before, though admittedly not often. And never like that... The memory of his lips on hers, so suddenly and surely, and the extraordinary way she'd felt... "What? I'm sorry. What did you say?"

"I said did he take you home, and did he kiss you?"

"Seretha!"

"Well, did he?"

Cara nodded, not willing to talk about it, even though she'd certainly been thinking about it. "The important thing is, how do you feel, Seretha?"

"That's not the important thing at all. I feel fine. You know I go through these little spells every so often," she said, each word an effort.

"I don't think this is just another of your little spells,

59

as you so lightly refer to them. I'm going to call Dr. Zylius." She felt a fresh stab of apprehension when Seretha's eyes closed and she didn't protest. "He'll come over and check your lungs."

Before Seretha could think better of her acquiescence, Cara went to the phone, thinking briefly that there probably weren't many doctors like Dr. Zylius left in America. Not only did he make house calls, but he treated the old ones as individuals, not as people whose problems and ailments were inevitable and necessarily caused by senility.

Cara managed to finish her duties after she put in the call to Dr. Zylius. She was pouring boiling water into Seretha's favorite teapot when the old lady said, her struggle to speak more obvious than ever, "I don't want to leave my home...."

Cara put the cozy over the teapot and went to sit on the footstool by Seretha's chair, taking her hand and holding it tightly. "You may have to, if it's pneumonia."

"I don't want to go," she whispered. "Couldn't you...wouldn't you be willing to take care of me?"

"Oh, Seretha, you know the answer to that! But I'm not a nurse, and it's highly likely you need hospital care for a while. If you do, I promise to look after your house."

"You will?"

"Of course, you know I'd do anything—"

"Would you move in here?"

"What?" Cara's eyes widened. "You mean sort of house-sit if you have to go into the hospital?"

"Yes!" For a moment Seretha's face had a bit more color, and it was certainly more animated. "For that matter, why couldn't you just stay on after I come home...if I have to go?"

"I hadn't thought of anything like that," she said slowly.

"Are you too attached to the cottage to leave it? If you are, I'd understand."

"As a matter of fact, I'm going to have to move in a couple of weeks anyway," she admitted.

Seretha's brief urge of strength ebbed away. She laid her head on the back of her chair and loosened her hold on Cara's hand. "But why?"

Cara stroked the blue-veined hand, mottled with age, with her own smooth, slender fingers. "Can't afford it for now. No matter how careful I am, there's always more month than money."

"I see." Seretha's breath was too shallow, as though she didn't have the strength to draw it deeper. "Then the arrangement could be advantageous to us both, dear."

"It might, at that." Cara had one ear tuned for the sound of the doctor's car, and she was relieved to hear a door slam and his hurrying footsteps outside. "But we'll discuss it later—"

"No! Promise me you'll move in right away, today."

"I...all right."

"Promise!" Seretha held her hand fast as the expected knock came at the door.

Dr. Zylius stood at the door smiling. His name was Lithuanian and he'd moved from his native Chicago to the tiny Oregon town by choice. He was a tall man with dark hair and a rather grand mustache that drooped a little. And his eyes were as fine and brown as Cara's own. Cara much preferred his navy beret to the ever-present baseball caps of most of the men around town.

"You said she's having difficulty breathing. Is it worse than usual?" he asked Cara as he rummaged in his bag.

She nodded. "And her color doesn't look good to me."

"Probably pneumonia," he muttered, a scowl on his rugged face. He wasn't a handsome man, but he had a certain appeal that couldn't be denied.

"I heard that." Seretha's breathy comment came from her chair. "You're just trying to frighten me, Dr. Zylius. Well, it won't work."

61

Cara followed him into the front room, hoping to keep the anxiety she felt from showing on her face. She was able to smile when the doctor, his stethoscope at Seretha's thin chest, said, "I'm well aware it won't work, Mrs. Hodges, because I tried already and it didn't." He was smiling, too, but Cara saw the look in his eyes as he finished his brief examination. "Get her ready, Cara. We'll just take her along in my car to the hospital." He turned to Seretha, whose crestfallen face was still. "If you don't mind my sweeping you up into my arms and carrying you out, that is."

Even with her breath in such short supply, Seretha could respond to him. "Mind? Why, Dr. Zylius, I'll be the envy of every female in Tillicum!"

With a sidelong glance at Cara he said, "Every one?" Before either woman could reply he said in a more businesslike way, "Let's get things organized, Cara, and get her to County General."

Half an hour later Cara breathed easier, knowing that Seretha was doing just that, breathing easier. Cara was allowed to see her for only a brief moment and was moved almost to tears at the sight of the tiny, frail woman enveloped in the oxygen tent.

"Get better fast, Seretha," she whispered.

"Take care of my house, my things...."

"I will."

"You'll move in now, and stay when I get home?"

The look on Seretha's face was compelling. Cara couldn't have denied her even if it hadn't seemed like a good idea. "I will."

"This very afternoon. Promise?"

"This very afternoon!" she said with a little laugh, knowing that quiet and rest were what Seretha needed most now. She squeezed her hand and mouthed a kiss, then left the room, only to almost collide with Dal Ross.

Dal had been waiting for her. He'd seen her go into Seretha's room and told himself he'd best check to see what the problem was. Before he could speak, she said in a mock gruff voice, "This town ain't big enough for both of us! Everywhere I go I run into you, Sheriff Ross."

"It's Dal, remember?" What he was remembering was the kiss that had accompanied the decision to call him that.

"Yes, I do. It must be the uniform that makes me feel I ought to address you properly."

"Oh? And what would you have me wear so that you'd feel comfortable calling me Dal?" He tried not to show how ill at ease he was as she looked him over from head to foot.

Neither of them noticed the two paramedics who'd overheard enough of the conversation to make them draw nearer, to hear the rest. "Um…" Cara said, "I think maybe Tarzan's loincloth might do it." She burst out laughing at the look on Dal's face, then heard the paramedics snickering.

One of them, whose name was Charlie, said, "I'd like to see that, Sheriff, you in a loincloth!"

"Don't worry, fellas, I'll sell tickets if he ever gets into one," said Cara. The two men went off down the hall, chuckling and glancing back every so often. Cara's expression changed as she said, "Sheriff…Dal, I'm sorry. I seem to have a bad case of 'hoof-in-mouth' disease."

He shrugged. "Those two make a second career out of looking for laughs." He was fairly close to her, but he put a hand on the wall by her head and leaned slightly closer. "Were your bruises and sore muscles from that little escapade the other day as bad as you thought they'd be? Surely that's not why you're here."

"I…um, well, I—"

She was so close to blushing, Dal couldn't help but smile. "You mean you don't know why you're here? Or did you forget?"

Cara put a hand to her cheek, then quickly took it away. "I'm here with Seretha Hodges. She had quite a severe asthma attack, and Dr. Zylius felt she should be admitted because of possible pneumonia."

"Dr. Zylius." His expression was thoughtful. "I've heard a lot of good things about him since he came to town. What do you think of the man? As a doctor, I mean."

"I've seen quite a bit of Dr. Zylius, and he impresses me more each time."

"Is that so? Well, he seems to be making a reputation for himself. I'm pleased when men of his caliber choose to settle in a small town like ours." He knew he was sounding pompous. Maybe this crazy girl was right, and he needed to loosen up.

"Sheriff, you aren't half as pleased as I am."

"I see." Dal didn't like the feeling that shot through him. He told himself it wasn't actually jealousy. It was more like...well, concern for Cara.

"Sheriff Ross, I—"

"I thought we had that settled. Or maybe there's some way I could convince you?"

"I can't say I'd mind."

Her little smile and his own memory of that kiss made him say, "I'll be off duty at five. Do you like movies?"

"I love movies!"

"Would you like to go with me?"

"Yes, I would, very much."

"Good. I'll pick you up at seven this evening."

"Oh, I'm really sorry, but I have other plans."

Dal couldn't help it; he frowned. "Dr. Zylius?"

Cara hesitated for a moment, then said in a rush of words, "I've never gone out with Dr. Zylius, mainly because he's never asked me, and if I gave you the impression that we were...that I...well, we aren't, and I don't!"

"I see. Then may I ask whom you *are* going out with tonight?"

She grinned. "You've lived here longer than I have. Surely you know how few eligible bachelors—at least

64

those within fifty-two years of my age—there are. The reason I can't go out with you is that I have to move."

"You're moving? Isn't this kind of sudden?" When she explained the circumstances, he was dismayed at the relief he felt. "Do you know anyone who has a pickup?"

"I've only been here a month," she said, shaking her head.

"Then how do you plan to get your things from one place to the other? And won't you miss the cottage?"

"In my car, and yes, a lot. Sheriff, you must be a master interrogator. You ask lots of questions."

He ignored her gibe. "You go on home and get packed, and I'll be over around seven with a pick-up." Without another word he snugged his hat on his head, turned, and strode away, leaving Cara staring after him.

In one way, packing wasn't hard; she'd only been in the cottage for a month. But she'd been very happy there and would have liked to stay. By the time Dal Ross knocked at the door, Cara had most of her packing done and all of her tears shed. She swung the door open, wiping her hands on the red paisley djellaba, a flowing garment that covered her from neck to bare toes. "Come in. It was really very nice of you to offer to help."

His glance swept to her pink-tipped toes. "It's cold. You should wear shoes," he said as he stepped in.

"You sound like my mother." Cara smiled at him, wondering if her delight at seeing him was visible in her eyes. "I guess it's a good thing I couldn't go to the movies tonight. We'd probably have a hard time finding one I'd like."

"Why's that?"

"Oh, I like the old ones." She was busy tugging at boxes, stacking them in neat piles. "You know, the ones where the villain always gets what's coming to him, and the hero's a real hero and gets the heroine, and everyone lives—"

"Happily ever after."

He took one of the boxes from her, and she looked at him keenly. "Do I hear a bitter note?"

His eyes were not on her. He was staring out the bay window that provided such a lovely view of the ocean. "Not bitter," he said, "just realistic. Not everyone finds happy endings."

"Maybe that's one reason I like old movies. Everything always works out, and people are happy with each other."

"That's just not the real world," insisted Dal.

She shook her head, gold-brown halo flying. "You've let your job get to you."

"Yours will, too, after a while. Have you faced the fact that you'll have to deal with more and more problems like the one with Mrs. Hodges today? That you'll even lose some of them eventually?"

Her chin lifted. "I don't think about it much."

"You'd better, or it will knock the pins out from under you the first time it happens."

Abruptly Cara changed the subject. "I've about got everything ready."

"Are you planning to go out in that rig?" His glance showed what he thought of it—which wasn't much. "It's cold out, you know. At least you'll have to put your shoes on." He looked around. "I should have brought someone to help with the heavy stuff."

"No need. Most of the furniture came with the cottage."

His eyes narrowed. "You mean to tell me you live in a furnished house? After that lecture about my apartment, I thought all this belonged to you."

She took his comment good-naturedly. "No, just a couple of the lamps and the blue chair and carpet. All of the books and plants are mine, too, and the kitchen kaboodle. And Miss Scarlett, of course."

"Miss Scarlett?"

"My cat. Well, she's pretty much my cat now, I guess.

The other day when I came home she was curled up in the window, looking in."

"So you brought her inside and fed her."

"Of course." She shrugged as if to say, *Who wouldn't?*, and proceeded to do surprisingly well at organizing the somewhat painful move.

It was only a few minutes after nine when they brought the last of her things into Seretha's lonesome-feeling house. "It's so strange without her here," said Cara, hugging herself. "I turned the furnace down when we left today."

"Want a fire?" Dal, his sleeves rolled up to his elbows, had shed his jacket earlier.

"Mm. That sounds nice." Cara shivered. She'd called the hospital just before they left the cottage, and Seretha was worse, not better. "I'm so worried about her."

He paused at the door. "As you pointed out, Zylius is a good man. He'll see that she's taken care of."

"Yes." Cara walked to the wide front window that looked out at the ocean. "I'll have to get used to another place, another bed. I'd just about settled in at the cottage."

"I'm sorry you have to leave it."

The rough sympathy in his tone touched her. "Why, Sheriff, I believe you are. I'll be fine here. The first night alone in a strange place is always hard, because you don't know if the creaks and moans are the house settling down to sleep or…*Something!*"

He laughed. "You're too fanciful for your own good. I'll bring some more wood in for you."

She chewed at her bottom lip, then said, "I suppose you have to leave after that."

"Well, it is after nine…." He trailed off, not really answering, and when he went out for another load of wood, Cara ran to find the *TV Guide*.

To her delight she found that *Rebecca* had begun at nine o'clock, and she knew there was some popcorn somewhere in her kitchen boxes....

The rose-colored sofa in Seretha's now cozy living room was covered in a soft, plushy fabric, and as usual, Cara's feet were bare as she sat back on them. The movie had just ended, the popcorn was all gone, and the fire had burned down to glowing, banked coals.

It had been an altogether pleasant evening, until Dal made the disparaging comment, "If that girl—whatever her name was, they never said that I heard—had had any backbone or had taken her head out of the clouds for five minutes, the story would have been over a lot sooner, and Manderly wouldn't have burned." He frowned. "And that guy got off. He *did* kill her, after all."

"Oh, that's the sheriff in you talking! Didn't you feel sorry for him? And why would you want it to end sooner?" Cara's wide brown eyes reproached him. "It's a wonderful story. I like it."

Dal rose and stretched. "That's probably because you're a lot like what's-her-name in the movie."

"Meaning?"

He smiled. It was the merest quirk of his mouth. "You'll have to admit, you don't live in the real world."

Cara stood up, her pleasure in the evening dimmed. "The real world, as you call it, is only as real as you'll let it be. What exactly do you feel you do to make things better?" For a moment he looked as though he were almost angry, which seemed too strong a reaction to her question. Cara thought that perhaps it was because he knew all too well how little he was actually able to do and because he felt frustrated and yes, angry, at his helplessness.

Aloud all he said was, "Thanks for the evening. I enjoyed...everything."

Feeling sure that he'd been about to say, "Being with

68

you," she wondered why he had changed his mind—*if* she was right. And then, because she never stayed serious for long and because she didn't want him to leave with any ill will between them, she said mischievously, "The movie, too?" Her grin was infectious, and she was glad to see his habitually somber expression lighten as she followed him to the door.

He opened it, but made no move to go. "I did have a good time, ah—"

She giggled, a tiny, bubbly sound. " 'Honey' sticks in your craw, doesn't it? Just say it. I promise it won't hurt…much."

"If I call you 'Honey' I might want to kiss you again."

"Suits me." She swayed nearer, her eyes meeting his, then closing as his head bent.

He touched her lips briefly with his. "Good night, Honey."

"Good night, Dal," she breathed, wanting the kiss to go on, to—But he didn't take her in his arms or touch her again. He just said quietly, "Lock up. I'll make sure the patrolman on duty checks the place a couple of times."

"I'll be fine." She shivered; the November wind was sharp and cold and laden with the sea.

"Go inside and put something on your feet, for heaven's sake," he ordered.

She nodded. She wanted to watch him go, but she obeyed rather than argue. The house seemed unbearably quiet and lonely now. Her earlier bravado faded almost completely as she went about straightening up.

It really wasn't a chore. Seretha's things were all so lovely. There was a dishwasher, but Cara knew better than to put the gold-trimmed china in it. She washed by hand the pieces that she and Seretha had used that morning. How long ago that seemed. As she dried and carefully replaced them in the corner cupboard, a prayer for her friend winged its way upward.

Later she picked her way through the maze of boxes in the room that was to be hers. She had already, during the homely task of washing dishes, begun her prayers. Cara rarely prayed on her knees; she prayed while she walked on the beach, while she did the dishes, while she brushed her teeth…

Her face in the bathroom mirror, toothbrush poised, stared back at her. *Oh, Lord, be with Seretha, especially through the night. Nights are when things seem scarier and worse. Help her to know how You love her…how I love her. Oh, God, I do!* The tears appeared suddenly. *And I love Tom and Mary and Virgil and…and—* She halted, well aware of the difference in her feelings toward Ladell Abernethy.

"Lord, I know You can change my feelings. I really want You to, and I give my resentment to You," she said honestly.

She shook her toothbrush and inspected her white, mostly straight teeth. They'd do for smiling. Her hair was bound up in a red bandanna for moving ease, and she slowly untied it and brushed her hair, head down. When she straightened, it stood out, looking like an amazing golden Afro, and she laughed. "No wonder that poky sheriff is leery of me!" Then she sobered. "He's not poky, and I'm sorry I said that, Lord. He's…well, You know what he is. And I seem to be falling in love with him," she admitted softly.

Cara drew on her favorite nightgown—her favorite one for sleeping, not going out. It was white lawn, sheer as a butterfly's wing, and had exquisite white embroidery all over the deep yoke and cuffs. "I've always believed You'd guide me to the right man, and I still do." Moving slowly, almost as though she were dreaming already, she made the single bed with clean sheets, then crept between their cold surfaces, and huddled until the warmth of her body seeped out.

"Be with me, and lead me. I love You...." Almost before she knew it, she was asleep. The wind shrieked and howled in a sudden squall a while later, and she never woke. The knowledge of God's watch-care—and that a patrolman had been alerted—was tucked deep in her subconscious. Her dreams were filled with a tall, dark man whose serious face only she could inspire to smile. The man called her Honey often and kissed her every time he did.

Chapter Six

Cara had plenty of things to keep her busy as the next couple of weeks slipped by. She made an order from the seed catalogue, thinking how pleased Mary would be, and settled into the beautiful house by the sea.

It was more of a pleasure than a chore to keep her promise to Seretha. Cara systematically dusted and polished and cleaned—from the china, crystal, and silver in the kitchen and dining room to the dainty Meissen figurines and hand painted vases in the living room and bedrooms. She found a great deal of satisfaction in caring for Seretha's lovely things, not the least of which was telling the older woman daily and in minute detail what she'd accomplished.

Seretha was improving, but her progress was slow. Mary Stewart, on the other hand, was pushing herself unmercifully in her thrice-weekly therapy sessions. She was now able to use a walker to drag her left leg slowly behind her, but she was adamant about not using the thing to walk down the aisle again in her beautiful wedding dress.

"I won't do it, Cara, not unless I can really walk!" she'd said passionately. Knowing how important the anniversary celebration was to Tom and Mary, Cara encouraged Mary every chance she got. She hid her doubts that Mary would be able to walk alone by December twenty-third.

Only two things marred Cara's days. One was Ladell Abernethy's stubborn resistance to Cara's every effort to befriend her. The other was the fact that although Dal Ross didn't seem to be avoiding her, his attitude was puzzling. There was a certain reserve in his manner that she couldn't figure out, especially after the evening at Seretha's. She kept thinking, hoping, that he would call and ask her for a real date. But he didn't. However, he seemed to turn up quite frequently where she was—at the hospital, where she went daily, sometimes twice daily, to visit Seretha; at the Senior Center, where she was organizing a talent show; and at Virgil's.

Dal just happened to be there at lunch time today, as he had two other times recently, and Virgil had said slyly, "You sure come over a lot more often than you used to, Dal." He glanced at Cara, whose face was rosy from the heat of the stove as she dished up the hearty chicken and dumplings. "It does an old man's heart good to think his only nephew is so concerned with how he's getting on. 'Course, if I didn't know you so well, I might think you had other reasons for coming." He stopped and sniffed appreciatively as Cara put a steaming plate before him. "Now it could be the food, I reckon." He glanced again at the silent Dal. "Yep, it must be the food."

Cara busied herself dishing up another plate, which she set in front of Dal. Badly wanting him to take up the teasing, she too stole a glance at Dal, but he said nothing. He merely shrugged, his face impassive.

Suddenly Cara felt a spurt of anger, thinking it was time she quit hoping and faced the facts. Dal had put locks on her doors, he'd come to dinner against his will and been embarrassed, he'd hauled her home after she'd made a fool of herself that day at Dead Man's Inlet, and he'd helped her move. Nothing there, certainly,

74

would give the remotest hint of grand passion. Just the sheriff doing his duty.

"Virgil," she said carefully, "if you're hinting around that your nephew is interested in more than my cooking, why don't you just ask him? Though I can tell you the answer." She met Dal's eyes squarely when he looked up at her.

"And just what do you think the answer to that question is?" His face had that somber, inward look that made him so unapproachable at times.

Cara's tone was deliberately light. "Oh, I'm sure as keeper of the law you have high standards for women, and any woman who'd wear her nightgown out in public might come up a bit short of the requirements in other ways, too."

Virgil's face screwed up in concentration. "You did that, wore your nightie in public?"

"She did." Dal nodded slowly. "Sit down so we can ask the blessing. I've got to get back to work."

"So we're on your schedule now," muttered Cara. But she sat down, relieved that the meal was eaten without further discussion of her peculiarities.

She knew, though, that no matter how pretty it was, the fact that she'd worn a nightgown out was far more important than the way she looked. Well, so be it. He wasn't the only man in the world, though she'd begun to think so; but no more....

Virgil broke into her thoughts with the casual comment, "I talked to Doc Zylius yesterday."

"About your heart?" asked Cara.

"No, about yours," the old man replied slyly.

"Virgil," she exclaimed, "have you been trying to match me up again?"

"Well, this nephew of mine seems to be kinda slow on the uptake. I thought a little competition might get him on the ball."

Cara, in the act of taking Dal's plate, was close enough to see the little scar at the side of his mouth.

And for several seconds longer than was comfortable, her eyes met his cool gray ones. She moved away, troubled.

"Virgil," she began, her hands busy stacking plates, "there's something you're going to have to face." Hearing the sound of a chair scraping the linoleum, she knew it was Dal's, and not Virgil's.

"Maybe you'd like for me to leave," he said.

"No, I wouldn't," Cara said as she turned around. Dal didn't move, but his watchful gaze warned her to be aware of Virgil's heart condition. "Don't worry, Sheriff, I won't upset Virgil. But he should know there's not the slightest chance you and I can…that we'll ever…" She faltered, then said, "I think it's obvious. Anyway, I've got to go as soon as these are done." She was scrubbing the dishes furiously, fighting tears.

"Hm." Virgil was no fool. He could sense that not only were the two of them not getting together, as he'd hoped, but there was definitely something very strained in the air between them. "Where do you go next, Cara?"

"Ladell Abernethy's, then the Stewarts'." She quickly dried and put away the dishes and soon had the kitchen spotless and in order. At the coat rack near the kitchen door she paused in the act of putting on her red tam and navy pea coat as Virgil asked another question.

"How're they getting on, anyway?"

"Fine. Take your medicine this weekend, Virgil. Don't forget." A wan imitation of a smile crossed her lips as she went out the door, leaving the older man staring reproachfully at the younger.

"Don't say it, Virgil," said Dal gruffly.

"What?" The injured look on his face was almost convincing, but then he blew it altogether. "You mean don't say, 'Go after her, boy; talk to her'? I wouldn't dream of it."

Dal retrieved his own hat from the rack and was out the door without allowing himself to reply. Cara was beside her car, its door open, but she was staring out at the sea. When she saw him coming, she started to get inside, but he was too quick.

His hand on her arm, Dal stood looking down, and now that he'd detained her he wasn't sure what to say. Her voice very low, Cara said, "I'll be late for Miss Abernethy's. And let me tell you, that wouldn't go over well." Her last words snagged on a breathy little sob.

"What's wrong?" His gray eyes held hers steadily.

"You don't know? You actually can stand there and tell me you don't know?" He shook his head, and she said, obviously fighting tears, "Let me go, Dal."

But instead of letting go, he caught her other arm and brought her even closer, forcing her to look up into his face. "Not until we get this straight. You made me feel lower than a snake's belly in there, and I don't like it."

Her eyes blazed. "*I* made *you* feel low? Do you have any idea how I feel?"

"No, I don't. But I'll listen if you'll tell me."

Cara wrenched away, her breathing shallow. "Whatever I do or say or wear, I have this feeling you won't approve. It's gotten to the point that whenever I go to my closet to get something to put on, I worry that the sheriff won't like it."

"You'll have to admit, you wear some wild getups." He eyed the fuzzy, hip-length brown sweater she'd paired with tweed wool culottes, and her favorite riding boots. It wasn't that she looked bad, she just didn't look...right.

"I don't have to admit anything. I like my clothes, and furthermore, I...I like myself! If you don't, that's your problem."

"I never said I didn't like you—"

"You don't approve of me. Try to deny *that* and I'll punch your face! I kept thinking you'd ask me out. I wanted you to, because I...I like you. And when you kissed me..."

77

"I'm sorry—" he began but she interrupted him again.

"This is no time for personal testimony! I've got to go. I'm already late, really."

He took a deep breath, willing his face not to show his struggle. "Maybe I'd better come by your place later so we can get this straightened out."

"I don't think there's anything to straighten out. There never was, and there sure can't be now." She got into her car and rolled the window down. Just before she started the engine she said, "Besides, I'm going home for the weekend. I need to be with people who love me, who think I'm fine as frog's fur!" And then she roared off, up the steep incline, scattering rock and racing the little Ghia's engine unmercifully. Dal was left with the sure knowledge that he'd botched things badly.

Cara wasn't late for her appointment at Ladell Abernethy's, but it was so close that the old lady had made up her mind the scatterbrained, sloppy Senior Services worker was *going* to be late. And in some twisted way, that's what she believed, no matter how Cara tried to convince her. In desperation, a few minutes after arriving, Cara brought the clock to show Miss Abernethy, who pounced victoriously. "See? *See?* It's after one o'clock, and you're supposed to be here at one!"

Still numb from her encounter with Dal Ross, Cara gave in. "I'm sorry, Miss Abernethy. It won't happen again, I promise."

"Well, see that it doesn't. I can't have you wasting my time, you know."

Cara started to ask her what else she did with her time but waste it, then clamped her lips shut after a tight little "Yes, ma'am."

For the rest of the visit Cara worked grimly and steadily. She accomplished a great deal even with Miss

Abernethy watching and criticizing every move she made. Relieved beyond words when it was time to go next door to the Stewarts', Cara said a subdued, meek good-bye which seemed to please the woman. Cara, however, was still seething when she knocked on the Stewarts' door.

Tom, wearing a soft, heather-blue turtleneck sweater that made his eyes look like the sea on a clear day, opened the door with a smile that went a long way toward healing Cara's wounded spirit. "Cara, come in! We've been looking forward to seeing you. Haven't we, Mary?"

Mary's smile was as warm as Tom's. "My, have we! Tom needs a…he's been trying to find a—" She stopped, the word she needed eluding her and the smile fading from her face.

Tom said a shade too brightly, "I want to make a quiche, Cara, but haven't the faintest notion how to start."

"Recipe!" said Mary as the word finally came to her. But there was no triumph; she felt the failure keenly.

Instinctively Cara knew the best approach was a direct one. "Mary, you're improving." Before Mary could protest, Cara shook her head. "The fact that the word came to you so soon is a good sign, and you know it. Sure," she added cheerfully as she began to tidy up the front room, "it'd be nice to remember immediately, but you're better now, and you're going to get even better."

It was what Mary wanted desperately to believe. Wistfully she said, "You sound so sure."

"I am sure." Cara whacked and fluffed the peachy-colored pillows on the blue sofa and placed them just so at each end.

"Do you really…do you believe I will walk by myself by Christmas?" Mary's voice held a naked edge of yearning.

Gruffly Tom said, "Well, if you can't, it won't be because you didn't try." He moved over to stand close beside Mary's wheelchair, the back of his hand brushing her cheek gently.

Touched to the core by the intimate gesture, Cara found herself a little choked up. It had been an emotional day. "I...I'll go copy off that recipe in the kitchen and make a grocery list." Cara went out into the compact little kitchen. Tom's basic sense of order helped enormously; everything was always in its place.

Seated at the table, she began the list. Nutmeg, for Tom's quiche venture, milk, ham, eggs...suddenly a thought intruded into Cara's mind, one which came often lately, no matter how much she pushed it away. She wanted a home of her own, a kitchen that *she'd* arranged and organized, and babies.

She felt a wry little inward smile at a flashed memory from her childhood: her mother tucking her into bed; the careful prayers including all relatives and acquaintances and pets, and then her mother, usually very perceptive, lingering. Cara had stared up into her mother's face, then blurted, "Mama, I want a baby!"

A little startled, Lexie Morgan had said, "One day you'll have babies, sugar. When you're old enough, you'll meet a wonderful man like your father, and he'll be your husband—"

"No, I don't want a husband," Cara had said matter-of-factly. "I just want a baby."

Her mother had gone on to explain how a baby needed two parents, a mother *and* a father, to grow up the way God intended, that one day Cara would change her mind and want a husband, too.

A huge sigh escaped her lips. Her mother had been right. Cara still wanted babies and a home of her own...but now she wanted a husband, too, a man who would love and cherish her and...

Tom's voice, so gentle and concerned, broke into her reverie. "Are you all right, Cara?"

That's what he's always saying, she thought, then made herself sound bright. "Of course, I am, Tom. It's

Mary who worries me. She's so totally set on walking without help by your anniversary. Do you really think she can?" She stuck the grocery list onto the refrigerator with a smiley face magnet.

"She wants to so desperately." For a moment his shoulders slumped and a frown crossed his face. "I'm afraid if she can't she won't allow the celebration at all."

"Oh, that would be terrible! Surely she won't call it off?"

He shook his head. "She just might."

"Wouldn't you be awfully disappointed?"

Tom took his time answering. There was a wonderful, faraway expression in his blue eyes. "I really would. But I have to consider Mary's feelings." He seemed about to say more, but Mary called out.

"Tom, the mail just came."

He gave Cara the smile she'd seen in the wedding picture, making her think it was certainly no wonder that Mary was so crazy about him, and went to get the mail. Cara had the kitchen sparkling when Tom came back in, a perplexed look on his face.

"What's wrong, Tom?" she asked.

"A package just came from the seed company."

"Oh, that's nice." She tried to act nonchalant and innocent.

"I don't understand. It's too early to be getting seeds, and I didn't place the order. Mary says she didn't either." He sat at the table and spread the packets out, looking interested regardless of whether he'd ordered them or not.

In her delight at his pleasure Cara forgot to guard her expression. "Are they the right kind? What do you usually plant? I thought maybe you could put a seed flat in that front window since it faces south—" Too late, she stopped.

He looked up. "You ordered them."

She shrugged. "Mary needs something to take her

81

mind off her therapy, something the two of you can do together."

"Thank you, Cara," Tom said humbly. "I should have thought of something like this." He grinned. "Maybe I'm just getting old and set in my ways. It doesn't occur to me to order seeds until after the first of the year."

"You can't think of everything, Tom. You already do more than most men would."

"I love her."

The simplest, most touching answer possible, it moved Cara almost to tears. To cover up her emotion, she began to inspect the little golden packets. "These carrots only get about two inches long. They're a new kind...fat, short, and sweet." She giggled. "Reminds me of my best friend at home!"

"Thank you, Cara. This could be just what she needs. There's something wonderful in watching seeds sprout and grow. It makes you feel hopeful...."

"I saw a book the other day at the library about apartment gardening. Everything in pots, stuff like that. I'll buy one as soon as I find it." She felt a sharp pang at the thought of what Mary's and Tom's marriage had been like before Mary's illness. It was what she wanted for herself, what her own parents had. Wanting to see them in their wholeness, she was impatient to be on the way home.

She finished up, pleased beyond words as she watched Tom and Mary deciding what they would plant where and making lists of indoor gardening supplies and grow lights. She had a list to check herself, and one thing she'd programmed herself not to forget was leaving out extra food for Miss Scarlett.

Grateful that cats were easier to leave behind than dogs, she checked on everything in Seretha's house, locked it carefully, and set off for her parents' home.

The drive to Salem took longer than Cara anticipated. It rained most of the time, and she had to drive more slowly than she normally would. But she enjoyed the deep forests on either side of the highway, enjoyed the welcome sight of the gently rolling farmland that was a sign she was close to home.

The Morgans had lived for most of their married life on several acres of land just outside of the capital city. Theirs was not a real farm, but it had been enough to keep them all busy even before Cara's older brothers, Jim, Dan, and Ted, had left the old place to make homes of their own. Cara's father had threatened to put the place up for sale when Cara "declared her independence" as he put it, but so far it was just a threat. Cara suspected that as long as he could manage the taxes, he'd keep the place.

As she turned into the drive that led to the house, she wished suddenly and fiercely that she were twelve and not twenty-two, that all her brothers were still at home and things were the way they used to be. Grandma would be waiting for her, gingerbread cooling on the table....She forced herself not to think of her grandma. If she didn't, she'd be bawling by the time she set foot in the door, and her mother didn't deserve that. She pulled her little car beside her dad's truck and cut the engine, telling herself home was home, and good any old way.

Her mother came out just then, a welcoming smile on her face. "Cara! You're just in time to peel the potatoes!" Enveloped in her mother's glad embrace, Cara breathed a sigh of pure contentment. Nothing was really changed if her mother was the same. Arms around each other's waist, they went in the back door. Mrs. Morgan said, laughing, "Remember when you were little and just learning to peel potatoes, and I always said—"

" 'I'll do it, Honey. I'm faster.' And I made up my mind I'd get to be faster than you, no matter what."

"Well, now you are, so get busy." She gave Cara one

last squeeze and went to the stove. "The potatoes are in the sink."

For a moment Cara feasted her eyes on the kitchen; it was the same, too. It had been added on to the house a few years ago, but it looked as though it had always been a part of the house. Mrs. Morgan had put a great deal of thought into making sure that it did. A large, square room with lots of windows on two sides and a skylight as well, it had butcher block counters, cabinets painted buttermilk blue, and blue and white checked gingham at the windows and on the round table in the center of the room. The hanging stained-glass light fixture above the table—a butterfly design with amber, blue, pale cream, and a touch of red—gave off a warm, inviting light.

Everything looked so cozy and familiar, Cara got a lump in her throat. To combat the threat of tears she attacked the potatoes with even more fervor than usual and sliced off one of her fledgling fingernails. However, she said nothing. She wanted to surprise her mother *and* Dal with real, paintable fingernails soon. As she made quick work of the rest of the potatoes, she was careful to tell her mother only encouraging things. Obviously pleased that Cara was happy in her work, Lexie Morgan listened attentively as she set the table, then poured two cups of coffee, and motioned for Cara to sit down opposite her.

Cara said brightly, "I moved a couple of weeks ago. I'm living with one of the ladies I work for, Seretha Hodges. She's in the hospital and asked me to stay at her place. It's a beautiful old house, with an ocean view."

"You didn't move because your finances are short, then?" Lexie Morgan had hazel eyes that changed colors according to what she wore and how she felt. Whatever color they were, they were always direct and honest, and there was no way anyone, least of all Cara or her brothers, could look into them and not tell the absolute truth.

Aware that she'd never deliberately withheld anything from her mother, Cara said slowly, "She's a very sick lady and she'll need someone with her when she—"

"Cara."

She gave up. "Yes, I'm a little short of money, but I'll manage."

"You know your father and I don't want you going without, Honey." Having worked her way up in her office, Lexie made a good salary, and together she and Cara's father made a comfortable living.

Ben Morgan walked in the back door just then, in time to hear his wife's quiet statement. He went to Lexie and gave her a squeeze and a kiss, but his eyes were on Cara. They were the same dark brown and wide spaced eyes as his daughter's. "So you came home to get refinanced," he teased.

"Daddy! I did not. I'm just fine, especially now that I've moved."

"Moved? I thought you liked your place, that it was your dream cottage." He went to the stove and sniffed appreciatively, then commented that the potatoes were boiling over. Both women scolded him and jumped up, then got dinner on the table a short time later. They'd always worked well together.

It was good being at the familiar table, even though it wasn't the same with just the three of them. Cara was both glad and sad that her three big brothers weren't there. She missed their fun and boisterousness, but not the merciless teasing they always subjected her to. And Grandma's empty place—better not to think about that.

Later they gathered in the family room, Ben watching television with his eyes closed as he always did, Cara and Lexie sitting in chairs drawn close together on the other side of the room so as not to bother him.

"Now tell me all about him." Lexie took a cautious sip of her herb tea, a new kind for them both, one called Red Zinger. "Mmm, good. Well, tell me."

Cara wasn't surprised that her mother knew there was a man in her life, even though there hadn't been all that many. Her mother seemed to have a sixth sense where her only daughter was concerned. Cara grinned. "You're like him in some ways."

"Oh?"

"Yes, he asks a lot of questions, too. He's the sheriff in Tillicum, and his name is Dallas Ross."

Lexie's brows raised slightly. "I find that interesting. I suppose he's a Christian, or you wouldn't even go out with him. But in a job like that, even a Christian can get disillusioned."

"In some ways he is, but in others, he's…" She trailed off, unaware that she'd breathed a deep sigh.

"That terrific, hm?" her mother said dryly. "How long have you been dating?"

"Mom, we aren't dating." Cara's answer was firm.

"But I thought you said—"

"He hasn't asked me for a date, not really."

"Well, why not?" Lexie's expression indicated that the sheriff couldn't be much of a judge of character if he passed up *her* daughter.

"I think he has a girl, and besides, he doesn't approve of me."

"What?" Cara's father sat upright on the couch. "How dare he not approve of you?"

"Now, Daddy, you'll have to admit I'm not everybody's cup of tea. Maybe I ought to…"

Her mother divined her unspoken thought. "Change?" Her hand covered her daughter's briefly. "Honey, I'll admit there've been times when your choice of clothes made me wince." She glanced at Cara's outfit. Loyally she said, "You look marvelous in brown. And besides, life will change you soon enough. We like you just the way you are."

From the couch came, "What I'd like to know is, do *you* approve of *him?*"

"Of course, Daddy. Dal Ross is a fine man."

"Just don't forget what your mother's always told you, Honey. You are the absolute best God makes, and you deserve the best man He makes." He scowled and lay down again.

Cara had heard that all of her life, and up until now she'd accepted it. How had her mother put it? *Cara, you're special and the best because of Jesus in you.* She felt better suddenly, and knew she'd been right to come home. "All this is slightly beside the point, anyway. Dal is definitely not interested in me."

"I wouldn't be too sure of that," her mother said thoughtfully. "He may just be playing a game."

"Men don't play games," muttered Ben, his eyes glued to the football scores on television. Both Cara and Lexie laughed, and he looked up sheepishly, then defended his statement. "Not the kind you're talking about, at least. Men are straightforward about relationships between men and women. You women are the ones who play games."

Lexie's brow was creased in a little frown as she repeated, "I'm not so sure. Cara, do you mind telling me whether or not you've indicated to Sheriff Ross that you'd be willing to go out with him?"

Cara made a funny face as she admitted, "I made it very clear that I'd like to."

"Maybe what he'd respond to is a challenge. If he thought you didn't want to go out with him—"

"No, Mom, you know me better than that. But it doesn't matter, anyway. I've decided he isn't right for me."

"You're sure about that?"

"I agree, Honey," put in her father. "He isn't good enough for you."

"I didn't say that," Cara frowned, trying to put her thoughts into words. "Dal is a good man, and he's very attractive. But I'm myself, and you've helped me see again that the man I marry—" She stopped suddenly. Remembering the style show and the song she'd sung, she rephrased her sentence. "The man I love will think I'm as nifty as I think he is!"

Lexie chuckled. Her voice was a bit like Cara's, deep

and husky. "That's my girl. This sheriff doesn't know what he's missing. There's something else on your mind, isn't there?"

Cara nodded and said wistfully, "It's neat to come back here, and things are the way I remember. But I'm ready for a home of my own and babies and—" She smiled, knowing her mother would remember, and said, "And a husband too, now."

"Don't be so impatient. It'll come. Try to enjoy this phase of your life. Now tell us about the people you're working with. Do you like them?"

"I love them, except for Miss Abernethy," said Cara with a wry expression. A few tales later, all three of them were doubled up with laughter.

It was her father who sobered first. "Just remember what the scripture teaches about love, Honeybun."

Cara stared at him. She had indeed forgotten. "Loving everybody doesn't mean we have to feel affection for them—"

"But it does mean the Lord intends us to do good to them, to want what's best for them," her father finished.

"Thanks, Dad, I needed to hear that," said Cara softly. "Oh, it's so good to be here."

"Want to move back?" Ben said, not bothering to keep the yearning out of his voice.

"I—no, I can't, Daddy. I need to learn to shift for myself." She flashed a grin at him and added, "With short trips home to juice me up, of course."

Gruffly Ben said, "I'm sending some extra cash with you. No," he said, anticipating her objection, "you have to let me do it, because I need to. Now you two be quiet, for heaven's sake, and let me watch the television in peace."

Cara blinked a couple of times and smiled through her sudden tears at her mother. It was so safe here, so good. God had richly blessed her in her parents. She knew she'd be ready to go back on Sunday evening and face all the challenges of her new life.

Chapter Seven

Because she never liked to miss an opportunity to see a sunset over the ocean, Cara made sure she left Salem in plenty of time to see what God was offering that particular evening. It was worth it. She parked at one of the highest lookout points and gloried in the blaze of color. The clouds were spectacular all by themselves, and the dying sun glazed them with a fiery purple which finally melted into soft, dreamy amethyst, leaving Cara wistful and dreamy, too.

Reluctantly she trailed back to her car, wishing she'd put on her heavier coat. The November wind had a sharp bite. It rarely snowed on the coast, but the relentless wind often made it seem colder than the thermometer showed. Cara looked forward to building a fire in the fine old fireplace and to making a cup of the good Red Zinger tea her mother had sent with her. Tonight she would plan her week. She told herself that life was full and right without the exasperating sheriff, that somebody better would come along. She chuckled softly. "How about soon, Lord? I think I'm ready for him."

Thoroughly at peace with herself and with the world, Cara drove down the steep road that led to Seretha's place. The isolation was part of the house's charm, no matter what Sheriff Dal Ross said. Cara chided herself; she was going to have to stop thinking of everything in relation to him. If it wasn't to be, it wasn't to be. God loved her and had someone for her, if she could just be patient. Patient. She'd never been long on patience.

The sight that met her eyes when she rounded the last curve in the road quite literally took her breath away. Somehow, though she never remembered doing it, she braked the car, turned the engine off, and got out, only to stand transfixed for a long, painful time. The beautiful house was reduced to a smoldering, blackened heap of rubble. A few upright supports were standing, like twisted black arms. The devastated mess was a sharp contrast to the dusky lavender sky and the clean freshness of the ocean beyond. The view that had been a joy before was now a mocking backdrop.

"*Seretha...*" A little sob tore at her throat. This house and all the wonderful treasures inside had meant everything to her! Tears, silent but painful, made their slow way down Cara's cheeks, and still she couldn't move. All she could think was, *Now Seretha can never come home, never.* Though she knew better, somehow the blackened, stinking wreckage took on an almost sinister cast, and Cara found herself shaking.

Suddenly a frightening thought struck her: Scarlett! Where had she been? Was she all right?...Cara began to call frantically and was glad beyond measure when the impudent cat came running, meowing her head off. For a few seconds she seemed bent on voicing her outrage at the whole terrifying affair. But Miss Scarlett quickly gave in to the lure of being cuddled and comforted, to the tender touch of Cara's trembling hand, the calming tone of her soft croons.

In her shocked grief Cara didn't hear Dal's car. She didn't hear his hurried footsteps or see the fierce scowl on his face as he saw her, shoulders hunched, clutching the tear-damp cat. "Cara...it's Dal." His hand on her shoulder was gentle.

Miss Scarlett jumped down, but she didn't go far as Cara turned and allowed herself to be folded into Dal's arms. "It's so awful...."

"I know." He held her close, his hand warm at the back of her neck. "I can't tell you how sorry I am you had to be alone when you saw it. I intended to be here, but there was a big raid this afternoon on some marijuana fields upriver. The state police call us when they're short-handed."

"It's all right." Cara's words were muffled against his coat. "How did this happen? And when?"

"I'll tell you, but not here." He started to lead her away, but she drew back.

"Then where?" Eyes wide with the sudden realization that she literally had nothing but what was on her back and in her car, Cara was almost shrill. "Don't you know almost everything I owned...*everything* Seretha owned, was in there?"

"Get hold of yourself, Cara."

Her head went up as a little spurt of anger shot through her. "Yes, sir, Sheriff! Don't worry, I'm not the kind who falls apart in a crisis. Scarlett!" She knelt and picked up the cat, who had stayed close, and started walking toward her car.

"Where are you going?"

His quiet, pointed question stopped her. "I...I guess I don't know."

"Get in your car and I'll drive you over to my place."

She felt his hand at her back, guiding her to the passenger side of her car. "What about...should you leave your car here?"

"I'll radio for one of the guys to pick it up. I go off duty in a while anyway."

"Oh." Feeling as though she'd relinquished all control to him and vaguely disturbed because of it, Cara nonetheless felt relieved at his taking charge.

Uppermost in her mind as he drove away from the ruin of Seretha's house was one question. She voiced it aloud. "Have they told Seretha? Does she know?"

His reply was heavy. "No, I don't think so, and the worst part of it is, I think Zylius had already told her she was well enough to be released in a day or two, since you're there...or would have been there." He took a long, deep breath. "I'm really sorry this happened." As though he anticipated her next question, he hastened to add, "Wait until we get to my place. Then I'll tell you the details. You need something hot to drink, a warm place. You're still shaking."

Numbly she nodded and was silent for the time it took to reach his apartment building. The fact that there was no view at all, much less an ocean view, barely registered. Even when she looked around and saw that the living room was probably exactly as it had been when he'd moved in except for an amazing number of houseplants, she couldn't summon the energy to comment. Beau padded in from the bedroom and wagged his tail in recognition, his eyes alight with interest as Scarlett made a low warning sound deep in her throat.

"Beau, behave." The big dog sank to the carpet at Dal's quiet command, but his watchful eyes were on the bundle held closely in Cara's arms. Scarlett was evidently intuitive enough to realize Beau wasn't a serious cat hater and settled down to the same wary watchfulness.

Still dazed, Cara sat where she was bidden, wrapped herself in the bright Pendleton blanket he placed around her shoulders, and accepted a mug of hot tea without words. But the question was in her eyes.

"It was vandals," said Dal.

"Vandals? You mean someone set the fire on purpose?"

"Sort of. We think they broke in Friday night, probably not long after you left the place."

She shuddered. "Were they from around here, or do you know?"

"The consensus of opinion is that they were just

passing through and…and saw you take your luggage to your car."

"They figured I was leaving for a while," she said slowly, following his reasoning.

"You were lucky."

"Lucky? How can you say that? Seretha's house and beautiful things, all my things—"

"You're lucky," he repeated, "that they weren't like that bunch we've been getting reports about."

"Which bunch?" Cara sniffed.

"The ones who seem to prey exclusively on women alone. They've raped and robbed and murdered their way across the western United States and are supposed to be in California right now."

"Oh." The word came out small. "It's still so awful I can't believe it."

"You'd better believe it, Cara. There are some scummy people out there, who not only don't care about you and yours, but think it's theirs if they can take it or spoil it." He sounded angry now. "We've got an APB out on them, but I doubt if we'll catch them. They're long gone, probably even out of the state."

Cara bowed her head and squeezed the poor cat, who squeaked her protest. "I don't want to think about it."

He stood up, a thoughtful expression on his face as he watched her. "I'll get some extra blankets. There's only one on my bed now, and you might be used to more."

"What are you talking about—my sleeping *here?*" she asked incredulously.

His gray eyes were unreadable. "Do you have a better idea?"

"Why, I—I could get a motel room."

"Do you have the money to stay in a motel until you get settled somewhere?"

He had her there and he knew it. She'd have to use the money her father had given her to replace her

93

household things. The enormity of her loss, of remembering that all her precious things were *gone,* hit her afresh.

"No, I don't. But I don't feel right about staying here, either."

"If you're worried about your reputation, don't be. I'll stay at my mother's until you can get a place. If I'm not mistaken there's a vacancy in this building." He went into the adjoining bedroom and was gone for such a long time Cara was beginning to wonder what he was doing. Just then he reappeared, a hang-up bag in one hand, shaving kit in the other. "I'll check on you early in the morning." A smile twitched at the corners of his mouth, the first since he'd found her. "Or are you a late sleeper?"

"I'll have you know I always get up early."

"Somehow I'm surprised. Are you sure you'll be all right here alone?"

"Of course I'll be all right. What do you think I am, a baby?" Cara stood up, then wished she hadn't, for he was closer than she'd reckoned. "I'll be just fine." Though she was determined not to back down from his steady gaze, it was Cara who looked away first. "Don't think I don't appreciate all this. I...I'll make it up to you."

"Oh, I'll see that you do, starting with your fixing breakfast tomorrow. Early to me is before seven."

"Fine." Cara ran her fingers through her hair. "How do you like your eggs?"

"Scrambled soft, with a little cheese grated in. And don't burn the toast. I put clean sheets on the bed. See you tomorrow, early." He stooped and stroked Beau's head. "He'll look after you." Then, before Cara could think of anything to say, he was gone with one last dry comment, "The door locks itself when I go out. That should make it easy for you."

And then she was alone. She put Scarlett down and was relieved to see that although the cat and Beau eyed each other for a minute or two, there seemed to be no real animosity between them. Cara and the cat made a prowling circuit around the apartment, Cara marveling that such a strong-minded man could make so little impression on his surroundings. Only the plants saved the place from total anonymity.

His plain contemporary sofa was upholstered in a plummy brown with two chairs to match. A dark coffee table and end tables with a benign ceramic lamp placed just so on each completed the furnishing. No pictures, nothing on the walls except a calendar and a large square mirror above the couch. She stopped and stared into it.

Her face was pale; her hair stood out like she'd stuck her finger in a light socket. Running her fingers through it again didn't help much.

Dal's bedroom wasn't much more personalized than the rest of the place except for one remarkable thing. There were, by Cara's actual count, fourteen paintings or prints of ocean scenes all around the walls.

But it was the picture of a small, dark-haired young woman standing beside a sober-faced Dal that drew Cara's eyes. *Love, Janet* was written across the bottom. She looked closely and saw that Janet was pretty and had an adoring look on her upturned face. With the feeling that she was being childish, Cara turned the picture face down.

There was a stack of books on the night table beside the bed, and, very much interested, Cara looked through them. They were all non-fiction, leaning toward biographies and histories, except for three police procedure novels, which tickled her for some reason. There was also a Bible, well-used and marked.

After brushing her teeth and washing her face, she put on her nightgown. As she crept between the sheets, she found to her delighted surprise that not only were they clean, they were warm. She switched off the lamp, and the light of the electric blanket control winked at her. A wry smile curved her lips. *People who sleep alone need a little help*....

Cara couldn't keep her wayward thoughts at bay. *What would it be like to sleep with someone...someone I loved, who loved me...someone who'd hold me close and warm...someone like Dal Ross?*...

She broke off in midthought, telling herself it was only because this was his room, his bed. But she wasn't altogether convinced. Knowing the only remedy was prayer, she whispered into the darkness, "Lord, tomorrow I'm going to have to face Seretha. I love her, and I know for sure that You do. I don't know what to say to her." She paused, then added, "You know my heart; You know my needs. Show me the right paths to take, and please, help me keep my thoughts right!"

Cara breathed deeply, enjoying the fresh, clean scent of the sheets—and something else, a hint of something that reminded her of Dal. She fought the rise of emotion at the thought of him and reminded herself of the smiling, dark-haired woman in the picture she'd turned face down. She made a silent resolve to fight the attraction she felt to Dal Ross, to subdue it entirely. Then, in an indecently short time considering the shock of what had happened, or perhaps because of it, she was asleep.

True to her word, Cara woke early the next day, six o'clock sharp as she always did. When she opened her eyes to the strange room with all the wonderful sea paintings on the walls, her disorientation was not quite as great as it could have been. But the shock of the remembered pile of burned rubble and its meaning for dear Seretha struck her anew. Through blinding, sudden tears she reached for Dal's Bible, grateful that hers was in her car, that she hadn't left it in Seretha's house.

Not sure what she wanted, she turned the pages carefully, noticing that Dal had marked many passages. One in Second Corinthians caught her eye, and she knew at once Seretha could use its comforting message, even more that Cara herself. Then, she saw that he had evidently found the same scripture in another version, for there was a scrap of paper tucked in, marking verses eight and nine in chapter four. "We are hard-pressed on all sides, but we are never frustrated; we are puzzled, but never in despair. We are persecuted, but never deserted: we may be knocked down but we are never knocked out!" Following the words of scripture was the note, J. B. Phillips translation. Her tears dried as she reread those verses and the ones following as well. Surely it didn't matter that Seretha's heartache was different from Paul's. *The same God comforts all doesn't He?* she thought. Feeling immeasurably better, Cara slipped from the bed, padded to the bathroom, and took a shower, during which she sang scripture songs at the top of her lungs.

Half an hour later—dressed in the brown outfit, for it was just about all she had—she'd fixed quite a presentable breakfast. She sliced the oranges and arranged them like sunny flowers on a plate and she had the toast perfectly done, the eggs just right when she heard Dal's knock. She dished out the food, satisfied with the way the table looked in spite of the fact that the dishes were pink plastic.

Feeling awkward to be inviting him into his own house, she covered it by saying sassily as she opened the door, "Hurry, Sheriff, or your breakfast will get cold!"

As he followed her into the alcove where the table was set, he said, "Did you sleep well? No nightmares about fires, I hope." His eyes took in the carefully set table which looked as inviting and fresh as the girl who'd already seated herself. "I could get used to this."

"What?"

"Having my breakfast fixed for me," he said, but his steady gray eyes were on Cara, not breakfast.

"Then maybe you ought to get married. Have you ever thought about it?"

He sat in the chair opposite her. "As a matter of fact, it

97

has occurred to me a few times lately." The last word was deliberate, and he met her eyes. "Are you in the habit of asking God's blessing on your food?" She nodded, and he reached out a hand to her.

She placed her hand in his and bowed her head quickly as he began to pray, his voice low and steady. "Lord God, we thank You for Your bountiful blessings, for this food, and...and for the hands that prepared it. Amen." It was a simple prayer, one which Cara had heard with slight variations many times. But when he didn't release her hand, just kept it clasped warmly in his, she raised her eyes to stare into his. "Cara..."

She held her breath, wondering what he was going to say. "What, Dal?"

He released her hand. "Your fingernails are looking a lot better. We'd better eat this before it gets cold, as you said before." He took a bite of his eggs and nodded approvingly. "Your car's outside. And I've already spoken to Mr. Detweiler, the superintendent of this building. He says you can have the apartment down the hall."

Feeling obscurely disappointed, Cara murmured, "Thank you." Just then Scarlett appeared at the window, meowing loudly.

As Cara rose to let her in, Dal said, "I talked him out of the cleaning deposit, but he wouldn't budge about the pet deposit. I take it he's had some pretty gruesome experiences with animals."

The cat stalked haughtily in, as though *she* certainly couldn't care less about rules and regulations. She also twitched her tail dangerously close to Beau's nose, but the huge, gentlemanly dog allowed the impudence. Worried now, Cara stood in the middle of the living room, watching the cat. "How much is it? The pet deposit, I mean."

"Seventy-five dollars," said Dal, finishing his eggs and a third piece of toast.

"Seventy-five dollars?" wailed Cara. "Plus the first

and last month's rent, I suppose. I...I can't manage that, not and eat, too!"

"Only the first month is due now. I vouched for your trustworthiness," he said with a smile. "Does that help? It's $275 a month, and believe me, you won't find anything much cheaper."

She nodded slowly. The cottage had been three hundred, and that had been more than she could manage. "I'll just have to find someone to take Miss Scarlett."

"You don't have to. I'm not crazy about cats, but I'd be glad to loan you the money." He eyed the cat, who had very carefully ignored him.

"No, I can't let you do that."

"Why not?"

"I told you before, I don't borrow. Maybe Tom and Mary Stewart will take her." She glanced at her watch. "I've got to get going. If I start early, I can be through at both Miss Abernethy's and the Stewarts' by the time they allow visitors at the hospital."

He nodded thoughtfully. "In case you're wondering, they haven't told Mrs. Hodges yet. You might check with Zylius."

"I will." She eyed the dishes. "Is it all right if I leave those until—"

"Don't worry about them. I've been doing my own dishes for a long time now, and my hands haven't fallen off yet. See?" He held both hands up in the air.

She stared at him for a long moment, thinking irrelevantly that he had nice hands. "You keep surprising me."

"Why? Because I do dishes?"

"No." She wanted to say that just when she thought he was one way, he proved her wrong; that she had resolved to fight the attraction she felt for him but wasn't sure she could. All she said was, "I'd better get going." She gathered the cat up into her arms.

"Don't be stubborn, Cara. Let me pay the pet fee."

She shook her head. "But thank you for everything. I really mean it."

He gave her a long, appraising look. "I know you do. See you later." He began gathering up the dishes then, whistling a tuneless ditty he'd heard at Virgil's.

When Cara arrived at Ladell Abernethy's a bit later she knocked, cat in arms, and stuck her head in the door. "Miss Abernethy? It's Cara. I have to go next door to the Stewarts before I—"

"What? I can't hear what you're saying! Come in here."

"But—" Cara gave Scarlett a careful squeeze and whispered, "Behave yourself, you hear?" The only answer from Miss Scarlett was a low growl of indignant protest.

"In here, Miss Morgan," came the command from Ladell Abernethy's bedroom. When Cara appeared at the door, that redoubtable lady, ensconced in a nest of lacy and crochet-edged pillows, said, "You're early." She made it sound as though this was as much a crime as being late.

Cara stifled a sigh. Late—early—never just right. But she heard her father's words as though he were speaking now. *You don't have to feel affection, Cara. Love is doing good to people, looking out for their best interests....* "Are you feeling all right, Miss Abernethy? Can I get you something?"

Looking as though a struggle were going on in her mind, Ladell Abernethy hesitated, then said, "I am a bit under the weather, Miss Morgan, and…and yes, a cup of tea would be nice." Cara nodded and turned to go. "What's that you have?"

Not wanting to go into the whole awful story of Seretha's house, Cara said, "I found a cat…I thought the Stewarts might want her. I'll just run over and ask—"

"Not on *my* time, young lady. I'd like that tea, and now."

"But Miss Abernethy—"

"Just put the thing down. It's housebroken, isn't it?"

"Yes, she is, and her name's Scarlett." Cara let the cat down, and as she left the room, hoping for the best, Scarlett began her tour of inspection of yet another new place, seemingly not nearly as displaced as Cara felt.

When Cara returned ten minutes later with an attractive tray of tea and toast, she was horrified to see Miss Scarlett snoozing at the foot of Ladell Abernethy's bed...*on* Ladell Abernethy's feet, to be exact. "Oh, I'm so sorry. I'll take her over to the Stewarts right now!" But when she settled the tray over the woman's lap and reached for the cat, Miss Abernethy stopped her.

"You don't have time now. I'd like you to begin your duties immediately so you won't have to rush so." As Cara went out the door on her way to hurry up and do her work more slowly, Miss Abernethy went on crossly, "I didn't ask for any toast."

Cara started to say that she would take it back, but noticed it was half-eaten. She solemnly said instead, "I'll be back later for the tray," then hurried out, glad to be able to do her work at her own pace without the watchful, critical eye of Ladell Abernethy on her. It would have been a pleasure if she didn't keep seeing Seretha's face, imagining her feelings when she found out about the fire.

The thought occurred to her that Seretha would feel even more displaced than she did and her heart was heavy with the knowledge. Had it not been for the sound of Miss Abernethy's voice just then, she might have given in to a fit of tears.

"Miss Morgan! Are you going to wait until lunch to take this breakfast tray?"

She hurried in, thinking she would probably have to encourage the woman to get out of bed and dress if she wasn't actually sick. If she was sick she'd have to be persuaded to let Cara call the doctor. Pleased, Cara said, "I'm all through—"

"Through? Impossible!" But even after a careful tour Miss Abernethy couldn't find anything wrong. She met Cara at the door, where she stood with Scarlett in her arms again. The scowl on the older woman's face deepened. "The Stewarts can't look after a cat properly."

"Oh, I think—"

"Mary Stewart can't even look after herself now."

"But Mr. Stewart—"

"Men hate cats!"

Knowing that wasn't true, but not really certain about Tom, Cara said, a little desperately, "But, Miss Abernethy, I have to find a home for her."

"Leave her here."

"Here? *You* want her?" Cara's wide eyes stared at the old woman, whose scowl had deepened by the second.

"Of course I don't want the silly animal. But it's the only neighborly thing to do." As if she had to do it before she thought better of her decision, Miss Abernethy reached for the limp, willing animal. As Scarlett nestled in the cradle of her arms, one thin hand went almost involuntarily to scratch behind Scarlett's ears. "I suppose you don't have any food for her."

"Yes, I do. I bought it on the way here this morning." Before Miss Abernethy could change her mind, Cara retrieved the food from her car, selected two dishes from the cupboard that finally suited both cat and new mistress, and left, amazed and pleased and incredulous all at the same time.

Chapter Eight

Cara had just finished her work at the Stewarts' when she heard a knock at the door. Since Tom was with Mary she went to answer it. The sight of Dal standing there, hat in hand, gray eyes steady and warm, lifted her heart. "How glad I am to see you!"

"Really," he drawled. "Well, I just thought you might like a lift over to the hospital. It's my lunch hour, and I need to check on a fellow there, too."

She squelched her impulse to ask why and to remind him that her car was outside. "Thanks, I'd appreciate the company. Facing Seretha isn't going to be easy."

"Who is it, Cara?" called Tom.

"Sheriff Ross," said Cara.

Tom appeared beside her. "Sheriff, how are you?" His smile was wide. "There's not a day goes by that I don't think about you, every time we use that ramp you built for Mary's chair."

Dal inclined his head a bit and said, "How is she these days?"

"Better, better," was Tom's hearty reply. "Come on, while Cara gets her things together, I'd like for you to see something."

As Cara went to the kitchen to get her coat and shoulder bag, she heard Tom's enthusiastic presentation of the gardening project. Later in the car, Dal cast a sideways glance at her. "So that's why you're short of money. Do you often do things like that?"

Cara shrugged. "Did you see how it's caught Mary's imagination? Tom says it's the first thing that has since the stroke. It's something they can do together, too, and seeds growing and changing can be the most fascinating thing in the world."

"All that stuff must have cost some," he said as they neared the hospital.

"Not nearly as much as a ramp." Then, dismissing both projects, she said, "But I'm still worried about their anniversary party. Mary says the whole thing's off if she can't walk alone by then."

"Think she'll be able to?"

Cara made a little hands-up gesture. "I really doubt it. I'm afraid she's pushing Tom right out of the picture. She's not really thinking of him or of what the anniversary means to them both."

"They're a fine couple," he said as he pulled up at the emergency entrance. "They were friends of my parents before Dad died and Mother started gadding about so much. I always thought Tom and Mary were the perfect pair."

"They still are. And Mary will see what she's doing. I'm sure she will." Her hand on the door handle, she stared moodily out.

"You don't have to be the one to tell Seretha about the fire, you know. Let Zylius."

Cara ducked her bright head for a moment, then lifted it and gave him a brilliant smile. "Thanks for bringing me."

"I'll park and meet you inside."

Without speaking Cara nodded and got out, not looking back, her mind on the task ahead. For she knew that unless Dr. Zylius had already told Seretha, which she doubted, it was up to her. *Lord,* she prayed, *give me the right words....*

Seretha was much, much better. But as Cara sat on

the edge of the bed and listened to the older woman's soft, excited words, she kept thinking of what Dr. Zylius had said just outside the door. "Cara, she has to go to a nursing home regardless of whether or not she knows about her house. We can put off telling her. In fact, when I talked to her son on the phone this morning—"

Eagerly Cara had broken in. "Is he coming?"

He'd shaken his head. "I'm afraid not. And he said to just put her in the best facility available and keep telling her she isn't well enough to go home."

"Keep lying to her, right?"

"That's a harsh way to put it."

"But it's the way it is." Abruptly she asked, "What do you recommend, Dr. Zylius?"

"If she were my mother I'd tell her the truth, let her start to face it now."

"And get on with her life. Her son obviously feels Seretha's life is over, doesn't he?—that it doesn't matter because she's old." After she'd left the doctor and headed for Seretha's room, Cara had breathed the same brief prayer...*Lord, give me the right words, please....*

There was no easy opening. Seretha was saying now, excitement making her normally pale face glow with color, "I can't tell you how much I'm looking forward to having you live with me. I know you love the house, too. Dr. Zylius says I can leave the hospital in a couple of days."

Cara held the thin hand that clutched hers a little tighter. "Seretha, there's something I have to tell you."

Seretha's breathy laugh was gay. "You broke something! Well, Cara, it happens." She was sitting up, propped by a couple of pillows, her blue eyes bright. "Come on, confess."

"Oh, Seretha," said Cara miserably, "I wish that's all it was."

The happy look faded. Seretha's eyes were still and watchful now. "Is it my son?"

"No, no, he's fine. In fact, Dr. Zylius told me he called this morning. And he…he agrees the best thing would be for you to go into a nursing home when you're well enough to leave here."

"Cara, aren't you still willing to stay with me?"

"Yes, but—"

"No buts. I'm going home!"

"You can't. I'm so sorry—you can't." Cara's brown eyes stung with unshed tears, but she'd have died before she cried.

"But why not?"

The soft, pained question pierced Cara's heart. Feeling Seretha deserved the truth, she forced herself to say, "The house burned, Seretha. Some transients broke in and started a fire in the fireplace. There was a flue fire, and…and it burned to the ground."

"You weren't in it?"

"No, I went home to my parents' for the weekend, remember? We…I thought it would be all right."

"Thank God you weren't there."

Cara knew Seretha meant the words, but she also heard a deep desperation in them. "I can't tell you how sorry I am."

"Of course you are. You're a very feeling young woman." Again, there was that awful sound of desperate pain. "Where are you staying, dear?"

A ghost of a smile lightened Cara's face. "Would you believe I spent the night at Sheriff Ross's place? He stayed at his mother's house, of course."

The faded blue eyes showed a flicker of interest, but it was over in an instant. "Of course."

Stricken by her friend's expression, Cara leaned over and hugged her. "I wish there were something I could do."

"There's nothing, dear." Her tone indicated there was nothing anyone could do. "It's…everything is gone?"

Cara swallowed at the naked hope she heard. "Everything. It must have gone up very quickly. It's so isolated, and no one saw the fire until too late."

Seretha's eyes closed and didn't open again. "I'm really very tired, Cara, dear. Would you...do you mind coming back later?"

"You know I will." She squeezed the hand she still held, but there was only the barest hint of response. She kissed Seretha's soft, wrinkled cheek, then tiptoed out of the room.

Dal was just outside, his face even more serious-looking than usual. "The door was open," he said, his eyes searching hers, "and I heard you tell her. But her voice was too low....How did she take it?"

Cara marveled for one brief second that he seemed to include himself so easily, then accepted it. She certainly needed someone to talk to, someone interested and strong and caring.

She shook her head slowly. "She was so quiet about it. I don't know what I expected, but I almost wish she'd cried and screamed and carried on."

He put an arm around her shoulders as they walked down the hall. "She may later, so be prepared. It must have hit her pretty hard. That's a tough thing to face." He stopped walking and looked down into her eyes. "And it was a tough thing for you to tell her, especially when you didn't have to."

She saw a mixture of things in his calm gray eyes—admiration, sympathy, and something else that made her heart trip faster. "I did have to. There really wasn't any other choice."

"Oh, some girls your age might have made an entirely different choice."

"I'm not a girl; I'm a woman."

The low, intense words hung in the air. "Maybe." Then, his eyes still holding hers, he said, "Would you like to go out for dinner tonight?"

"With you?" She laughed. "Let me get this straight. You are actually asking me for a real, true date?"

"I may retract the invitation," he said, scowling now.

"Oh, no, don't. I accept. But I don't have anything to wear." She looked down at the brown outfit.

"What about buying a new dress?" he suggested. "At a new store?"

She laughed again. "I like to eat too well for that. Nope, this is it, unless you count my jeans and flannel shirt. That's about all I have at the moment." She caught sight of Dr. Zylius just then and missed the look on Dal's face. Even if she'd seen his expression she couldn't have deciphered his feelings. He was having some trouble sorting them out himself.

After discussing Seretha's state of mind with Dr. Zylius—and to her surprise, turning down *his* offer to take her to dinner that evening—Cara met Dal at his car and they headed to Virgil's. As she got out of the car, Cara asked Dal, "What time shall I be ready this evening?"

"How about six-thirty?"

"Fine. See you then."

"Come in this house, Cara-Honey!" Virgil held the door open wide, his eyes delighted. "It's not my day. Why're you here?"

From the first, Cara had instinctively known two things about Virgil Penhollow: he felt things deeply, and he'd never learned to show it. Now, following her intuition, she took a step closer, put her arms around him, and hugged him tightly. "I just needed to see a friend," she said simply. He couldn't quite bring himself to put his arms around her, but he certainly didn't pull away, either.

When she drew away and took off her hat, she noticed a suspicious wetness in the corners of his eyes, but he turned and went to the kitchen, calling back, "Come on in and sit a spell. I'll make you a cup of java that'll kill you or cure you. Rough weekend, huh?"

Cara sat in the chair she habitually took, not stopping to wonder at the reversal in their roles. If she'd been more experienced, she probably would have known how good it was for Virgil to "do" for her, but Cara knew only that she needed what Virgil had to offer…friendship. Virgil's need to offer it was beyond her at the moment. Head on her arms, voice muffled, she said, "I can't begin to say how hard it was for me to tell Seretha about her house being burned."

Virgil's hand hovered briefly over her shoulder; then he moved around to sit opposite her. "Must have been," he agreed. "It's a good thing she wasn't in it, is all I can say. And you too, Honey."

She looked up. Unlike Dal, Virgil seemed to have no trouble whatever calling her that. She decided she'd given in to her maudlin feelings long enough, and her eyes glinted mischievously. "Did you know I spent the night at Dal's apartment last night?"

His look of shocked surprise made her laugh outright. "You did, you say? What…um…" He stammered a little, then said, "Are you funning me?"

"Would I joke about something like that?" she asked, big-eyed.

"Then you're lying! You're not the kind of girl who'd…ummm, well, anyway, Dal's too proper."

"You're absolutely right." Cara decided to put him out of his misery. "He spent the night at his mother's, Virgil. He was just being nice."

"About time," grumped Virgil, stirring his coffee furiously. "After the other day I thought the two of you had declared war."

Cara was gazing out the window. A gull beckoned to her from the mostly blue sky. She needed a long, long walk on the beach, but there would be no time today. Somehow she had to get together enough things to set up housekeeping in that dreary little apartment. "I thought so, too, but would you believe he actually asked me for a date this evening? He must feel sorry for me."

Virgil's bushy, gray brows lifted. "Don't be too sure about that. Maybe there's hope for him yet."

Shyly Cara said, "Hope for me, you mean."

"Like him, do you?" His gnarled, work-worn hands were flat on the scarred surface of the table before him.

She reached over and put both her own hands on his. "I do, Virgil. He's everything I ever wanted in a man." She thought of Janet Moody and said slowly, "It's just that I'm not—"

"Don't you dare say you're not good enough. You're as fine as God makes, and don't forget it."

She grinned at him. "That's what my dad always says."

"Your dad's a lucky man, having a daughter like you," he said gruffly.

Restlessly, Cara got up to see where the gull had soared. "Wouldn't it be awful if I died an old maid?"

Virgil's snort of laughter made her turn quickly as she realized what she'd said—and to whom. "There's worse things, girl, and I'm the one who knows all about that particular subject."

"Oh, Virgil, I'm sorry."

"Don't be. Sure, sometimes I regret not marrying, but I just never found a woman like you who'd have me." His face sober now, he added, "It's not dying without ever marrying I think about now. It's…it's just dying, period."

Cara went to him and dropped to her knees. Always direct, she whispered, "Are you afraid, Virgil?"

He took his time answering. "I'm not sure. It's not what comes after that's worrying me, not that I got the slightest idea, even after reading the book of Revelation from start to finish." There was the hint of a smile on his mouth now. "In fact, I might know a bit less."

Cara had felt the same way herself, but she didn't want to discuss the mysteries of Revelation now, and she didn't think Virgil did either. "What is worrying you?"

He looked down into her brown, serious eyes and knew she cared deeply. "I'm not getting any better, Cara. I'm getting worse almost every day. It hurts to walk, sometimes even to breathe. I'm afraid."

"Of what, Virgil?" she whispered.

He shook his head, and it took a long time to get out his next words. "I'm afraid I'll die like a coward, sniveling and crying from the pain, not like a man!"

"Oh." The soft word from Cara's lips was almost lost in the intensity of emotion in the room. Realizing how very much it had cost him to admit it, she wanted so badly to help him that it was like an ache in her breast. As her mind searched frantically for an answer, her heart sought God without really knowing it. Then she said, with quiet fervor, "Once, when I was probably only eleven or twelve years old, my parents took me to a revival service. They were always making us kids go with them, and I didn't want to go. I wanted to go skating with my friends." He smiled a little, and she prayed consciously in her mind then for the right words. "I didn't hear everything the preacher said because I was mad at being there. But he said something about dying grace…and it caught my attention because I had an Aunt Grace."

Again he smiled, bemused by her. "But he wasn't talking about your Aunt Grace, was he?"

She shook her head. "No. And I'm still not sure what all is involved, but he said that if we belong to God, that when it comes time for us, when we—"

"When it's time for us to die," he supplied gently.

"Yes, when it's time for us to die. I guess what he was saying was that most of us don't know much about dying grace because we don't need to know about it until we need to have it." She had a thoughtful look on her face now. "Grace. It sort of means a gift from Him that we don't deserve, I think. But He gives grace to us because He loves us. Virgil, you *know* He loves you, don't you?"

Slowly he nodded. "I know it."

"Then believe that He'll give you a special kind of grace when you need it. He will!"

111

Virgil stared into her glowing face as he repeated, "He will." Again that slow nod. "Thank you, Honey."

She got to her feet and placed a light kiss on his cheek. "He promised never to leave us, didn't He?"

"Seems like I remember reading that."

"Then wouldn't He be with us especially at that time, when we have to face the unknown, and we're alone?"

"You are so right it makes me ashamed of myself— you being so young and all. I've been a believer for a mighty long time, too. Gave my heart to Him when I was a young man." A regretful look came onto his face. "But I always thought working was the most important thing, that God understood when I was out on the boat on Sundays."

"He did," Cara said gently.

"Sure, I reckon He did. But it meant I never worshipped like I should have with folks who believe the same as I do, never got to grow much as a Christian."

"It's never too late to grow!"

"You think not?" Her enthusiasm plainly tickled him, but he looked doubtful.

"Do you read your Bible every day and worship in church now?"

"Have been lately," he admitted.

"Then you're growing, and if you read it believing, He'll give you light. It's true," she insisted.

Virgil was grinning widely now. "You're the beatingest girl I ever saw. If Dal doesn't see how fine you are, he's hopeless."

Cara refused to think about that now. "Virgil, would you like to pray with me?"

The surprise that flickered for a moment in his eyes was replaced with gratitude. "That'd be good, Honey. But could you? I've never done much praying out loud."

"Sure I will." Her hand on his shoulder, her eyes tightly shut, Cara prayed, as she always did, in simple, direct words. "Dear God, show Virgil every minute, every day, how much You love him. Let him know deep in his heart that when…when his time to be with You gets here, You won't let him make the journey alone, that You'll give him grace." She was silent for a long, breathless moment; then she whispered, "Amen."

"Amen," echoed Virgil, not ashamed now of the tears streaking his face. "Amen."

Suddenly Cara said, "I'm about to starve to death! Is there anything to eat in this place?"

"Uh, I dug some clams this morning," he said, watching her face shyly. "Chowder sounds nice, doesn't it?"

"Chowder?" wailed Cara. "I'm sick of chowder! Let's go to the Dairy Queen and have hamburgers with everything on 'em and wonderful greasy French fries and strawberry milkshakes."

He grinned. "Sounds good to me."

"It does?" Cara covered her surprise, determined to hustle him out before he changed his mind.

Cara dropped Virgil off later and reluctantly went to the small apartment. In her mind its only asset was the fact that Dal Ross lived down the hall. And she was beginning to wonder how she'd manage to get the necessities she'd need, much less clothes.

She found a note on her door from Dal saying that they were going on a picnic so her jeans would be fine to wear and he'd pick her up at six-thirty. He was prompt, but Cara was ready long before he knocked. She met him at the door, jacket and hat in hand. "You're all ready," he said, as though he were surprised.

"I've been ready for a long time," she said, laughing. "You'll have to admit there's not a whole lot for me to do here. I don't have many clothes to choose from, so it didn't take me long to decide what to wear."

She passed very close to him and paused just a moment before they went out. His eyes met hers and she saw something there that made her say softly, "Where are we going.…For the picnic, I mean?"

"You'll see—one of my favorite spots since I was a

113

kid." Outside the sky was clear, the cold air smelled of woodsmoke and sea. There was no wind. "A perfect evening," Dal said with satisfaction as they got into his car.

"A perfect evening," she echoed, feeling a strange, sweet excitement stirring within her. The resolution to fight her attraction to Dal retreated far, far back into her mind.

A couple of hours later she had to admit that so far, it had been just that, a perfect evening. They'd spent the better part of the first hour on the beach gathering firewood, then building a glorious bonfire that warmed at least one side of them at a time. The wind had been steadily rising, and a bank of low thunderheads was gathering from the horizon, but they'd roasted wieners to a charry perfection and eaten innumerable hot dogs, not to mention half a bag of marshmallows.

Cara was laughing now and carefully toasting the perfect—she declared—marshmallow, after a series of blackened ones that she'd eaten anyway, to Dal's derision. He *was* rather good at it, as he smugly proved over and over. "Wait," she cried, "this one is better than your best—" She snatched it triumphantly away from the glowing coals at the edge of the bonfire and took it from her stick, offering it to Dal, who shook his head.

"I'm full," he groaned.

"Oh, come on, no fair! You just don't want to have to admit I can do one as well as you can." She took a bite; then, to her chagrin, the puffy brown morsel dropped to the sand. "Now you'll never have to admit it—" She stopped suddenly. He had caught her elbow and was pulling her down, and she found herself on the sand beside him.

"Cara," he said softly, just before his lips found hers. The kiss was light at first. It wandered from her mouth to her throat, and back to her mouth.

It was as though she'd never been kissed before. The depth of feeling he aroused in her—that she gladly al-

114

lowed him to do—was such that she began to shake. "Oh, Dal," she murmured, her lips still captured by his.

"You have the sweetest mouth." Once more he kissed her, exploring its softness.

Suddenly Cara said, "It's the marshmallow." Laughter lurked in her words.

"What?" He drew back slightly, but he didn't release her. His hands were at her waist, holding her close.

"I told you how good my marshmallow was."

He stared at her for a moment in the firelight; then he laughed, too. "Oh, no it's not. It's you." Then, as if to make absolutely certain, he kissed her again and again.

It was only when they felt the sting of rain, sharp cold drops driven by a sudden squally wind blowing in from the sea, that they broke apart. "We'd better run for it!" Dal gathered up the basket. "It's a good thing we put away everything but the marshmallows."

Cara, still breathless from his kisses, grabbed the half-full bag, and together they began to run. Only a short distance down the beach they came to a driftwood shelter that some ingenious kids must have spent hours building. It was about six feet long and not that high, but sturdily built. Dal pulled her toward it. "Come on, we can wait out the worst of it in here."

One end had been left open to form a door of sorts, but they had to duck to get inside. Luckily the wind was coming mostly from the other side, which was solid. A huge log was shoved against the back; perhaps the kids had even built their "fort" around it. Dal pulled her down onto it beside him. She noticed that his head nearly touched the top of the structure. Shivering, she tucked the marshmallows into the basket he had dropped on the sand, then said in awe, "Look, it's like a picture window...."

Visibility was fairly low, of course, because of the lateness of the hour, but the view of the crashing turbulent seas was still awesome. The white foam that frosted the wild waves seemed more beautiful against the darkness, and the sound of the ocean in turmoil was thunderously musical to Cara. "It's so beautiful I want to cry."

"What did you say?" Dal pulled her closer, his arm tight around her, his lips on her jaw. When she repeated her words he said, "I know. When I was a boy, this is where I came when I felt rotten, or when I felt terrific. No matter how I felt, it was better for me here. I guess the ocean speaks to me."

Cara gazed out at the dark beauty of sea and sky. "Maybe it's God speaking."

With one finger he turned her face to his. They were inches apart, their eyes straining to see in the dimness. "Maybe. I believe you understand."

"I do." She closed her eyes, intensely aware that he was going to kiss her again, wanting it more than anything she'd wanted in her life.

Cara knew she should ask Dal about Janet Moody now, before things went any further. But she didn't, and for a very good reason. She didn't want to know.

The storm raged outside, but the storm within Cara made it fade away. In those moments, although she certainly didn't stop to analyze it, she committed herself to the man whose arms held her, whose mouth claimed hers.

Chapter Nine

"So, where are we going?" asked Cara, feeling a delicious, double dose of excitement. She loved going "junquing," and she loved being with Dallas Ross. "I've noticed a couple of neat-looking shops around town."

"I thought we'd go up to Newport."

Cara would have much preferred staying in Tillicum, but since Dal had been thoughtful enough to suggest and plan the outing—and the bare little apartment was about to drive her crazy—she didn't object. Instead she said shyly, "The other night was wonderful. You sure know how to plan a picnic." Her tone turned mischievous. "And you're a real connoisseur of hot dogs."

"You mean I like them charred like you do," he replied dryly. "It's the only way I can eat the things." He made a disgusted sound. "Some people boil them at home and actually think they're edible."

"Nasty." Cara laughed. "The fact that we both like charcoaled weenies cooked—on an open fire—"

"On the beach," he joined in, and she met his eyes briefly.

"That must be very significant," she finished. To herself she added, *Like we're meant for each other....*

He couldn't take his eyes from the road for long since they were on a stretch that curved like a snake with a bellyache. But the frequent glimpses of the ocean were

117

like gifts from the Father. As they wound between the high, rocky walls on either side of the highway, an occasional break would provide a spectacular view of azure water with long, white frills on each comber. The brilliant blue sky met the water on the far horizon and mirrored the blue of the sea.

It was an absolute dazzler of a day, a day that gave lavishly of its mood to Cara. Dal slowed as they approached an S-curve and glanced at her. "You look especially pretty today."

The casual compliment made Cara's heart soar. "Thank you. Aren't you awfully tired of all the variations of my brown outfit? I am."

Dal was, too, but he wasn't about to say so. "I think it's not what you're wearing that makes you pretty, but how you feel. Why, if you didn't have on anything at all, I imagine you'd still look great."

"Why, Sheriff, I didn't know you were the kind to think such things."

"I just—" He realized suddenly what he'd said, and to Cara's delight, he flushed a dull red. "I didn't mean...."

Cara clamped a hand over her mouth to stifle the laughter, but it didn't do much good. Finally she gasped, "Oh, Dal, you *are* human! Isn't that neat?"

He rolled his eyes, still embarrassed. "Neat. Now, what I meant to say was—"

"I know what you meant," Cara said softly, thinking that his hair was a beautiful color, that she liked the shape of his sideburns. "And I wasn't making fun, no matter what it sounded like. I'm tickled to death to see a different side of you. I want to see *all* of you—"

He roared with laughter. "*Now* who's human?"

She laughed too, so happy, that the moment was like a sweet pain. When the laughter had left them breathless she said, "Did you hear the one about the woman who, after she and her husband had been married several years, told him one time as they were driving down the road, 'We used to sit close.' He looked over at her, crowding the other door, and said, 'Well, I haven't moved.' " Cara slid over until she was near enough to touch her shoulder to his. "Do you mind?"

"No, I don't mind." He was looking straight ahead, and his tone was low. "But there's a seat belt for the middle, and I'd feel better if you put it on."

"Always practical," Cara said lightly, and she buckled up. "Now tell me about this place we're going to. You say it's an old hotel?" The nearness of his body distracted her. She kept thinking about how the warmth of his arm and thigh felt against hers. His description of Newport's best second-hand shop, an old hotel, barely penetrated the yearning haze that claimed her for the remainder of the ride.

They spent the better part of an hour browsing through the seemingly endless little rooms of the hotel, each one filled to capacity with collectible trivia. Cara stayed longest in the big old kitchen, regretting anew the loss of her lovely old green glass dishes as she saw the awful prices on these. Carefully she selected an assortment of kitchen utensils and enough dishes to serve two—not green Depression glass, not fiesta ware, just someone's castoffs. Placing her choices on the counter in the "lobby" for safekeeping, she and Dal then made their way through the large room which held mostly furniture.

She stopped beside a worn, comfortable-looking Morris chair. Its once-maroon upholstery was now sort of liver color. She sat in it, then got up and motioned for Dal to try it. "You may visit sometime, and I want you to fit in my only comfortable chair. The ones in the apartment must be left over from the Inquisition."

Though he looked doubtful at first, he had to admit that the chair was comfortable, even as long-legged as he was. She dropped to her knees on the floor beside him, and their eyes were almost at a level. "Cara, maybe

119

you should consider buying a new chair on credit. I'd be glad to cosign if you need it, and you could arrange for monthly payments you could afford."

She wore the brown and red and gold paisley scarf tied pirate style on her head today. Her fluffy curls stood out around it like a slipped halo. "Dal, in the first place, I don't like new furniture, and in the second, I once attended a financial freedom seminar with my parents."

"I have a feeling I'm about to get one of the guy's lectures."

"Well, he made a lot of sense, even if I didn't learn as much as my folks did—"

"Daydreaming, I'll bet."

Cara ignored him; she had been. "But I remember one thing that really seems to make a lot of sense the older I get."

"And what's that?" Dal's look was one of amused tolerance, mixed with that certain expression that made Cara's heart trip faster.

"Never buy a depreciating item on credit."

For a moment Dal frowned; then he said, "I never really thought about it, but I guess I can see the wisdom in that."

"Sure, I told you it made sense. Television sets, boats, cars—why do you think I drive that old Ghia? These days most people can't buy a house without borrowing money, but houses appreciate. And things like…like babies. I guess you could say babies appreciate. Say, do you want children?"

He took his time answering. "Yes, I do." Then his eyes crinkled, and the smile reached his mouth. "You're quite a girl, Cara. You surprise me. To look at you, it's hard to believe you've got—"

"Sense? Oh, I've got enough to get by."

"I believe you do, at that." His steady gray eyes took in the slender figure, the polished riding boots, her scarf-wrapped head, the bright, lovely face. "You'll make some man a fine wife."

Cara took a deep breath, not breaking the contact of their eyes. "What kind of woman do you want to marry, Dal?"

He shrugged. "I always thought I wanted a woman who's old enough to know who she is, who wouldn't be threatened by my job…a woman who could be at home in all kinds of situations and take care of herself in them—I guess someone who's realistic about herself and her world."

That doesn't sound very much like me, thought Cara with a sinking sensation. *I wonder if it sounds like Janet Moody….* "You like the chair, I can tell. So I'll buy it. The other reason I buy old furniture is that you can always recover it, which I'm learning to do, by the way. The new stuff just isn't built as well, at least not the pieces I can afford. Sheriff, can I buy your lunch? Anything but clam chowder!"

During lunch, which he insisted on buying after all, they talked of many things. Without seeming to, Cara drew him out about his preferences on everything from houses—"just so they're on the beach" was a preference that suited her very well—to liver and onions, which they both hated.

When he helped carry the last of her purchases and stood at the door of her apartment, he said, "I'd rather stay here or take you to my place."

"We've been together all day," murmured Cara, feeling exactly the same way.

He gazed down at her. "It doesn't seem to be enough."

"I know." Cara wanted to put her arms around him and hold him. She wanted to so badly, she found her hands in tight fists at her sides.

"I'm afraid if I kiss you I won't be able to stop."

"We could try and see," she whispered.

He laughed and caught her to him, burying his face in

her hair. "Your hair is so soft, and it smells nice." His lips found her temple, her cheek, then her lips. "One, just one."

But to Cara's intense satisfaction it was a long one. When he broke away and went down the hall without speaking another word, she stood staring after him, her mouth tender from the kiss. He paused at his door and looked back for a second. Cara laughed. "You're supposed to say, 'Here's looking at you, kid,' like Bogey." He shook his head and went into his apartment, closing the door. Cara did the same, wishing for the feel of his arms, his lips on hers again. She sighed. The nights seemed to be twice as long since she'd met Dal Ross. And she'd long since forgotten that resolution to fight her attraction to him.

The next day was so full that even though she and Dal were neighbors, she didn't see him all day. There were her regular duties with the Stewarts and Miss Abernethy—who was almost being nice. Cara attributed that to Miss Scarlett's good influence. She also had a talk with Mrs. Lane, her supervisor, about finding someone new to work for in place of Seretha. The idea hurt, and Cara was determined to be there when Seretha was transferred from the hospital to the Care Center. The news about her house had set Seretha back quite a bit; she'd had to stay in the hospital several extra days.

After three o'clock, breathless and late, Cara arrived at the Care Center. She inquired at the desk about Seretha and was told how to find her room. She'd fully intended to be here before now, to make sure it was a good place. *And what if you decided it wasn't?* she thought to herself as she made her way down the hall. *You're not her daughter, after all. What can you really do for her?* Out loud, Cara added fiercely, "Love her!"

At least someone had taken care to paint the walls a nice shade of creamy ivory, and there were plenty of windows. She saw what looked like a sun room off to one side, and the plants were all healthy, their green-ness giving a pleasant feeling.

Seretha's room was the last one on the left. When Cara knocked gently, then pushed open the door, she had to work hard to keep her shock from showing in her face. "Seretha! It's so good to see you."

Only it wasn't. Fully clothed, Seretha lay precisely in the middle of the made-up bed, as though someone had placed her there. When she saw Cara her lips smiled, but her eyes didn't. "Cara. How nice of you to come."

"Nice? *Nice?* Nice is for people who don't love you. I do!" Cara went to her and laid her head on the frail, flat old chest. *I will not cry*, she thought. It took a few moments to ward off the tears. When Seretha patted her a couple of times, it was even harder, but Cara finally raised her head, her eyes dry. "I'm sorry I wasn't here when they brought you."

"It's all right."

Perched on the edge of the bed, Cara eyed Seretha. "Your hair needs setting, and you don't have any make-up on. Where's your kit?"

Seretha shrugged. "It doesn't really matter."

"Yes, it does, too." Cara hopped off the bed and went to the bureau. There in the top drawer was Seretha's blue-flowered make-up kit, her toothbrush, and an extra nightgown. Cara had packed them in the rush to get Seretha to the hospital the day she'd been so terribly sick.

"That's all I have in the world, Cara."

The low bitter sound of the words shocked Cara. She picked up the make-up case and walked slowly back to the bed. As she got out the mirror and all the things she knew Seretha used, she said, "I can imagine how you must miss your house, your things." She gave a jar of face cream to Seretha, who took it, opened the lid, and began to rub it into her face almost as though she were unaware of doing it.

"Everything gone, everything." The pain in her voice was echoed in her eyes.

"Dal and I...we can look for some new things for you, some things to brighten up this place." Cara glanced around at the neat, bare little room.

"It wouldn't be the same." Seretha was making slow, upward strokes. "You can't possibly understand how precious my things were. You're so young."

Cara bit her lip. She thought of all the things of her mother's that were burned in the fire. The quilt her grandmother had been given when she taught in her first school, and had given to Cara when she left home. The round gold watch that had been her Aunt Annie's, the lovely little satin glass lamp her mother had cherished. Aloud all she said was, "It must be hard. But you're strong, you'll be all—"

"No, I won't be all right! I don't like it here. I don't understand why I'm here, why God allowed this to happen to me!"

Shocked, Cara swallowed hard. Her mind worked frantically, searching for the right words. When nothing came, she said, "Here, let me show you a new way to fix your hair." She brushed the limp, faded hair gently and twisted it in an intricate, high knot on top of Seretha's head. Then she took the paisley scarf from around her own head and tied it around Seretha's bun, the ends sticking perkily out the back. "There," she said triumphantly, reaching for the mirror. "How do you like it?" Seretha stared into the mirror, her eyes signaling her anger and pain. Before she could say anything, Cara, who'd been rummaging in the make-up case, said, "Let's try something with your eyes. Hey, look at this. What'd they do, give it to you when you bought something else?" She held up one of those kits that department stores sometimes give away with a large purchase. It was a palette of eye colors, a regular smorgasbord of choices.

Seretha had a slightly glazed look in her eyes; she said nothing, hardly moved, as Cara gently, carefully—and with no small amount of skill—applied make-up to the sad old face. Cara's experience in little theatre stood her in good stead now, and she kept up a running commentary about her date with Dal and their excursion to the antique shop in the old hotel in Newport. Then, almost before Seretha knew what was happening, Cara had her up and in front of the big mirror. "Look at that. Are you a knockout, or are you a knockout?"

Seretha stared at her reflection. "I...I do look better."

"You bet you do. And when we get back from the sun room, I'll give you a lesson." Before Seretha could protest they were out the door and halfway down the hall.

In the sun room a woman who introduced herself as Nell, said to Seretha, "You look different. What'd you do?"

Seretha's reply that Cara had done her make-up made Nell say, "Could you teach me how to do that?" Another couple of the women chimed in, and one brave man ventured the comment, "Sure wish some 'em could learn to look better, or get in a supply of paper sacks."

That started a lively spate of mostly good-natured jibes back and forth. Cara circulated, telling them all to go and get whatever make-up they had, that the next time she came she'd bring more.

For the better part of the next hour almost every woman in the home took a turn in front of Cara's improvised make-up table, and she marveled inwardly that they were almost like a bunch of teenagers at a slumber party. They were delighted when Cara promised to gather together a lot more beauty tips and paraphernalia, and come again for another "beautification session." The women wandered off, mirrors in hand, preening like peacocks.

Finally, Seretha, whose face was a bit more relaxed, a little less unhappy, said to Cara, "Can you stay for supper?"

The hopeful look in Seretha's eyes made Cara regret

that she had to say, "I'm sorry. I can't. The talent show is tonight."

"Oh." Seretha couldn't quite stifle a sigh. "I wish I could go. Are you going to sing?"

"Well I did practice a song," admitted Cara as she sorted the make-up and put her own back in her bag.

"Will you sing it for me, please?"

Cara couldn't refuse. She stood up and hugged Seretha's frail body, noticing with a sinking heart how much thinner the bout with pneumonia had left her. Her arm around Seretha's shoulders, Cara walked with her to the piano in the corner of the sun room. She thought briefly and with deep regret of Seretha's fine old square piano and hoped her friend wasn't thinking of it, too. As she sat down on the bench and opened the piano, Cara was glad to see that it wasn't as bad as some she'd played. She ran up and down a scale or two, then tinkled out the melody. Though she wasn't an accomplished pianist, she could get by.

With a simple introduction, she began to sing, smiling at Seretha, who'd pulled her chair close to the bench.

"It had to be you...." It was Dal who filled her mind as she sang. Cara knew she'd never sing a love song again without thinking of his dark hair, those gray eyes that could be as warm as the summer sun or as cold as a winter day. And his mouth...

Her daydream was shattered by enthusiastic applause as the last sweet note faded. When she looked around, all her prettily made-up new friends were clustered around, clapping and smiling.

"Do another!"

"Let's hear 'Bye, Bye, Blackbird'!"

Cara loved to sing; she even loved to perform, but only in certain settings. This was a perfect one. These people weren't critical, and they liked the same music she did. Without hesitation she launched into the song, encouraging them to sing with her, which they did almost without exception. Finally, laughing and breathless, she said, "Just a couple more. I really have to go!"

"When the Roll Is Called up Yonder!" Several more gospel tunes were named, and Cara played them mostly by ear, with more fervor than proficiency. She noticed out of the corner of her eye that Seretha knew the words of the hymns and all the verses and that she kept the others going. She also noticed that Seretha's face showed more animation than it had since she'd fallen ill. Seretha was better. "One more," Cara said, smiling.

"Amazing Grace" was the choice. Several of the older ones chimed in together. When the last notes faded, Cara rose from the bench and turned to face practically the whole population of Tillicum Care Center. As she and Seretha moved toward the hall, the residents begged her to come back. Cara couldn't help but notice Seretha's proprietary hand on her arm. It was as though she were saying, "Cara's *my* special friend, and don't forget it."

At the front door, her arm around Seretha's shoulder, Cara said, "I'll be back."

"Soon?"

"Of course. We'll fix your room up nicely, and—"

"It won't be the same as having my own things. I'll never see my house again." Her voice broke and Cara realized that although Seretha had forgotten for a time, she would never fully recover from the blow of losing her home. But Cara would do what she could and trust God to do the rest.

"Seretha, you're the one who kept them singing. I didn't realize you knew all those hymns by heart and could sing that well."

A little smile touched Seretha's mouth. "Before the asthma got so bad, I was a pretty good singer."

Cara hugged her tight. "If you were any better, I couldn't stand it! We'll work together, you and I. I need to enlarge my, um, repertoire?" She laughed and kissed the withered, but prettily rouged cheek. "You go through the hymnal and pick out some good ones. And…and I'll bring you a new Bible." Tears clouded Seretha's eyes, and Cara knew she was thinking of the Bible that had burned. "I wish so much I'd packed it with your things. I'm sorry."

"It's not your fault," murmured Seretha, struggling not to cry.

"Hey, didn't you tell me the print was too small anyway? I'll get you one with *B-I-G* letters!"

Seretha laughed in spite of herself at Cara's wide-eyed exclamation. "You don't know how much it means to me for you to come. It's…I feel like a stranger here."

Cara wanted to tell her that she'd settle in, that she'd make friends, that God would help her find her place here. But she just hugged Seretha tightly again and promised to be back soon. Then she left, knowing with a wisdom far beyond her years that, regardless of her feelings, only Seretha's attitude could make the difference.

Chapter Ten

As she made her reluctant way to her new apartment, it was her own attitude that concerned Cara. The place was so faceless, so dreary, with nothing there to make it her own except the few things she and Dal had gotten the other day. "It's a good thing Seretha can't see inside my head now. She'd tell me to keep my hypocritical advice to myself," Cara murmured as she fumbled in her purse for the door key. She saw the note then. It was short and very welcome.

"Come down to my place. I've got a surprise for you. Dal."

He opened the door at her first knock, a silly-looking grin on his face. She wanted to throw herself into his arms; instead she said, almost demurely, "It's so nice to see you." All the while she was longing for him to hold her close, to kiss her.

But he held her at arm's length, his eyes taking in her slim figure from head to toe. "It should fit."

"What should fit?"

He went to the couch and held up a dress, his face showing how pleased he was. "I bought you this."

"You bought me a dress?" she repeated as she took the dress from him. It was dark blue, some sort of silky-feeling fabric, and a size seven. "How did you know what size to get?"

"I sort of guessed from the way you felt." He was looking at her expectantly.

"It's very pretty." It *was* pretty, stylish, and very...right. A dozen thoughts buzzed in her brain. Shoes would be a problem. And she had no nylons, no jewelry, no proper coat to wear with it, no petticoat....The list seemed endless. For an instant she regretted not having friends her own age to borrow from. Maybe Mary would have something. "Thank you, Dal. It was very thoughtful of you."

"You like it, then? You'll wear it tonight?"

"Did you...were you planning to take me to the talent show?" Cara hated herself for the suspicion, but it lurked in her mind and wouldn't go away. He didn't want to take a chance on what she might wear if they were going to be seen together.

He nodded. "I thought we'd go out for supper in a little while, too. The Lighthouse."

Cara knew then she was right. The Lighthouse was not an elegant restaurant, but most of the residents of Tillicum went there regularly, and if Sheriff Dallas Ross took a date, who she was and what she wore would be discussed with no small interest around town. Though Cara told herself his feelings were natural, a tiny part of her mind resisted—but not for long. "How long have I got?"

"Can you be ready by a quarter after six?" His fingers brushed the silky fabric of the dress draped over Cara's arm, then moved to caress her arm lightly.

She glanced at her watch. "Oh! I'll have to hurry—"

"Then make it six-thirty. I'll pick you up." He walked with her to the door. "I think I'm going to like having you for a neighbor."

For a few seconds she stared up into his gray eyes, thinking how clear they were, how honest. He had dark lashes, almost longer than her own, and brows that he used expressively. Impulsively she stood on tiptoe and kissed the crooked little white scar near his mouth. "I like it, too." It was only half untrue; that dreadful apartment was the problem. Then she ran lightly down the hall, the dress fluttering, aware that he was watching. Remembering just in time that she hadn't locked her door, she shamelessly made a show of "unlocking" it and waved to him before going inside.

The Lighthouse would probably have been popular because of its decor even if the food hadn't been good. Not only was there a small revolving beacon light which was actually registered with the Coast Guard, but nautical paraphernalia adorned the walls—sextants, compasses, ships' lights, and brass instruments of all kinds. Someone had come up with the idea of carrying the light motif even further. There were binnacle lights, ships' cabin lights, lanterns, and lights for every possible use on the walls, on the tables, hanging from the ceiling. But someone had made quite sure that even with so many, the glow that emanated from them was soft and understated.

Cara watched as Dal hung her wrap, an outrageous cape she'd borrowed from Mary. He'd whisked it off her shoulders almost as soon as they entered the restaurant. She'd been taken with the cape, a dull satin thing that was sedate black on the outside, but lined with smooth satin as green as a colleen's eyes, as green as a shamrock growing in the heart of Eire. Mary bought it on a trip to Ireland a few years back and never had the courage to wear the dramatic, beautiful thing. Of course, it had taken Cara's fancy. But obviously not Dal's. As he returned she could almost see the relief in his eyes.

"You look very pretty. That dress becomes you."

She smiled over the implied "now" in his words, but she felt troubled all the same. There seemed to be a great many things Sheriff Ross didn't like. But all she said was, "Thank you." Impulsively she took his hand, hoping he'd notice her nails. He did.

He grinned. "You're really doing great."

"I certainly am. They'll be long enough to polish soon."

Slowly his gaze swept from her almost tame hair to the toes of her borrowed pumps. Mary had said to keep them, as well as the cape, but Cara wasn't sure she wanted the plain, pinchy things. As for the cape, she could see Dal wasn't too wild about it, but it didn't seem to matter as much when he said softly, aware that the owner of the restaurant was approaching, "That dress looks so good, I might have to pick out your clothes from now on."

Cara had mixed emotions about that. The thought of a future with Dal Ross certainly had more and more appeal to her. But for him to pick out her clothes...She was relieved when Mr. Bollinger, the restaurant owner, said grandly that he intended to show them to their table himself.

Dinner was excellent, and the service, impeccable. Dal was so attentive and obviously proud of her that Cara almost forgot the vague, nagging notion at the edge of her consciousness. But the feeling that she was playing a part kept creeping in, and at times she thought the strain must show on her face. In fact, as they were finishing dessert, Dal asked if something was bothering her.

"No, no," she said, acutely aware that it was not the first time that evening she'd felt as though she were hiding her feelings. "I'm just thinking about the show....I should be there early."

He nodded, accepting her explanation. "You wait in the vestibule while I pay the check."

Cara retrieved Mary's Irish cape and had it draped over her arm when Dal came up a bit later. "I'll just carry this."

He may have been tempted to let her, but he shook his head. "It's too cold for you to go without it." He took it and placed it around her shoulders, the high, double ruff framing her face. "It makes you look like a movie star, or...a princess."

"Is that bad?"

He didn't answer. His arm around her shoulders, they made a dash to the car, for it had started to rain. Cara told herself that they were all small things and not really important. But she was glad she would be too busy all evening to think about it.

The Senior Center was already crowded when Dal and Cara arrived, and they could sense the excitement as they walked in. As unobtrusively as possible, Cara slipped off the cape and hung it up at the door. Determined that Dal would be proud of her, she allowed herself to walk into the room with her hand possessively tucked into the crook of his arm. Cara was well aware that the raised eyebrows, the whispered comments, the bright, interested glances all added up to one thing: *Look who brought Cara!* Although she tried not to, she kept wondering if they were thinking about Janet Moody, too.

She peeped at Dal, knowing he, too, had to be aware that they were the center of attention. Just as he'd obviously known they would be. That brought her to the dress; he'd known, all right. She smoothed the silky fabric over her hips, determined to see the gift in the best possible light. After all, she was in desperate need of clothes....Her chain of thought was broken at Mrs. Lane's approach.

The woman's smile widened as she took in Cara's dress, the plain and proper pumps, the closely pinned hair. "Cara, how nice you look. And this, I'm told, is the sheriff."

Cara made the necessary introductions, then said, "It's good of you to come to our show, Mrs. Lane."

"Not at all, Cara, I'm looking forward to it. Sheriff Ross, I've been getting good reports about this young woman. She has a talent for her job, you know."

"Yes, she certainly seems to, Mrs. Lane," he said.

"In fact," Mrs. Lane continued, "we've been consid-

133

ering offering you a part-time position as coordinator of activities here at the Center. Would you like that?"

"Oh, Mrs. Lane, that would be the answer to my—"

Mrs. Lane nodded encouragingly. "Your prayers? Don't be afraid to speak out. In this business, prayer is sometimes all we've got." She waved at someone across the room. "We'll talk salary and what the job would involve later. But right now, I believe someone over there wants you, Cara. Leave your sheriff to me."

Cara nodded, pleased more than she could say about the prospect of getting paid for something she considered fun...and was already doing, anyway. She gave Dal's arm a squeeze and hurried off to get the show started.

And a very good show it turned out to be. Beginning with a man who claimed to be ninety-six years old and who played a wonderful harmonica, it progressed to a bluegrass fiddler ("*not* a violinist," he solemnly proclaimed), a trio of women who patterned themselves after the Andrews sisters, a tap dancer who could have given Fred Astaire fits, and finally, to a newly formed "orchestra."

This last act consisted of Mrs. Johnson, an enthusiastic piano player, the bluegrass fiddler, a sad-faced little man who played a happy mandolin, and to Cara's absolute delight, a bass player who had ingeniously devised his own instrument: a number two wash tub sprayed gold, with a mop handle—head still attached—as the upright to which the lone string was fastened. Somehow, though the exact logistics escaped Cara, he could loosen and tighten the string in tune, and he twanged it with gusto and perfect rhythm. The music the little quartet played was so happy and infectious that several couples pushed back their chairs and got up to dance.

Although each act had only been scheduled to perform one number, the Old Gold Tubbers, as someone dubbed them, responded graciously to about fourteen requests, and the number of dancing couples increased with each one. Even Dal presented himself to Cara with a murmured comment about this being different from the dancing everyone did nowadays.

As they circled the room, Dal's hand at her waist, a decorous five or six inches between them like every other couple around them, she said, "Of course it's different. People used to show respect for each other whether they felt like it or not. The way the dances are now, it's just the other way around."

A smile crinkled his eyes. "You mean nobody shows respect whether they feel it or not? Sick."

"You said it. Of course, I'd rather have someone respect me *and* show it."

He was gazing down into her eyes; he'd also stopped dancing. "You mean if I held you close, it would show I didn't respect you?"

"Oh, I don't think I meant—You're teasing, now."

"Sort of. But I'll have to admit I'd like—" He was interrupted by Otis Monroe, the man who'd volunteered to emcee the show. Otis's voice came booming out over the mike.

"Let's hear it for the Old Gold Tubbers!" He started the applause himself, and the crowd took it up enthusiastically. He finally had to lift his hands to quiet them. "Are you ready for our favorite singer?" Again, the applause was long and enthusiastic, for they all knew whom he meant. "Cara Morgan, who thought up and put this show together. And it's been real good, hasn't it? Let's show her how we feel about her!"

Cara made her way through the people and felt their warmth in the comments and pats. As she stood before the microphone, waiting for Mrs. Johnson to play through the introduction, she couldn't help but remember the last time she'd sung. Then, she'd been certain Dal wasn't in the audience. Now, she knew exactly where he was, and as she began to sing, it was straight to him, every word meant for him alone.

It had to be you, it had to be you,
I wandered around, and finally found,
That somebody who
Could make me be true,
Could make me be blue....

Cara saw Dal grin, knew *he* knew she was singing to him. With a little toss of her head she sang huskily, until the last note gave away to wonderful applause. She loved it and told them so, but declined to sing another song even though they begged her to. All she really wanted to do was be with Dal. Chiding herself, telling herself she ought to keep her mind on her job, she was still hard put to do so. She was glad to see Tom and Mary Stewart and went over to speak to them.

"Mary! How did your therapy go today?" Cara missed the quick frown on Tom's brow until it was too late.

Mary's face, animated at Cara's approach, grew still. "All right."

Tom said, a little too heartily, "The big news is about Ladell."

"Really? What happened?" Cara asked, thinking that Mary's therapy must have hit a serious snag.

"She's actually come outside two days in a row."

"You're kidding!" Cara's eyes widened; it was a well-known fact that Ladell Abernethy hardly ever left her home for any reason. "Why?"

Mary's face lost its pained look. She even grinned. "Miss Scarlett mustn't be allowed outside alone, Honey. Surely *you* didn't let her? If you did, for heaven's sake, don't tell Ladell!"

"Don't worry. I won't." She laid a hand on Mary's shoulder. "I'm just glad the two of them took to each other." Her eyes searched the crowded room.

"He's over there, by the kitchen door," supplied Mary gently. "You two look like an 'item,' as we used to say."

"Mary!" scolded Tom, but his gaze on her was fond. "Don't tease her."

"It's all right, Tom. We aren't—" Cara caught sight of Dal then, as he came out of the kitchen, coffee mug in hand. "Excuse me, will you?"

"I sure will," said Tom. "Fifty years is not so long I don't remember the feeling I see on your face."

"Now who's teasing her?" Mary said.

"I'm not teasing," Tom said. "That's the absolute gospel truth. And don't tell me you've forgotten."

Mary squeezed Cara's hand, but she was looking up at Tom when she said, "I haven't forgotten. Cara, keep us posted. We're interested. You know…we really care about you."

"I do know, Mary, and I'm grateful. See you later." It took Cara a few minutes to make her way across the room to Dal and every time she glanced his way his eyes were on her.

His first words were, "That was quite a performance."

"Did you like it?" Cara wondered if he was going to ask if she'd been singing to him, but he didn't say anything for a long time.

"Yes," he said finally, "I liked it. Say, when can you leave? It's noisy in here, and I'd rather hear the ocean instead."

"That does sound marvelous. Just give me a few minutes to make sure everything is taken care of."

"Ten, no more." He was almost smiling; his face had that thoughtful speculative look he sometimes got.

Her own smile was dazzling, and she made her good-byes sweet and short. The thought of the water, the wind, and the wide dark sky…with Dal…was like a siren call.

Dal had promised to take her to a lookout point she hadn't seen before, and by the time he finished winding slowly upward, meandering around and around on the narrow road, Cara was really looking forward to the view. "It must be spectacular."

"It is. There's even a little stone structure at the top. If it were daylight I'd show you some of the botanical specimens they've got labeled. There are quite a few nature walks with information placards all along the paths."

"I'd like that," said Cara, thinking she'd like almost anything so long as she was with Dal Ross.

"There are a lot of things in the area I want to show you." He navigated the last turn, a particularly sharp one, and pulled into the deserted parking area. Before Cara could slide over and let herself out of the car, he was out and halfway around, his intention clear. As he opened her door and took her arm, he said, "You look so nice tonight you make me feel like a gentleman."

Though she enjoyed the attention, Cara couldn't help saying, "So, if I had on one of my funky junque-store outfits, you'd let me open my own door?"

He put his arm around her waist. "Of course not. It's just that, well, I've thought a lot about why you don't dress the way—"

"The way I should."

"That's not what I was going to say."

He sounded troubled, and Cara's natural receptiveness to people's moods made her soften. "I know you're just trying to help." The wind hit them suddenly as they came out of the shelter of the tall firs edging the parking area. Cara welcomed the sharp coldness. She didn't want a direct confrontation with Dal, or worse yet, an argument. "Besides, you said yourself the other day that it's what a person is inside that makes the difference, not what they wear."

"I said that?"

"Sort of."

He stood behind her and pulled her close to him as they reached the rock wall which defined the path at the top of the steep cliff. "Sounds better coming from you. And this view is unbelievable when you can see."

Cara leaned back against him, loving the warm strength of his body. "If it were any better I couldn't stand it," she murmured, not meaning the view at all. The ocean's roar was muffled from this height, but the feeling that they were on top of the world, on its very edge, heightened her joy at being so near him.

"Are you about to get settled in your apartment?" asked Dal, his arms crisscrossed around her, his fingers clasping her waist.

It was obvious to Cara, even though they were so far above the water, that a storm was brewing; she could see small jags of lightning flashing low over the water, seeming to connect ocean and sky. She considered giving him a polite reply, then decided she cared enough for him to trust him with the truth. "Oh, Dal, no. I don't like it at all, and I find myself making excuses not to go there—I can't even call it home."

"Hm. That's not good." He kissed her neck softly, and when she shivered and pressed closer, his lips were against the softness of her hair as he murmured, "Do you want to find another place, to move?"

She turned suddenly in his arms, her hands on his shoulders. "Do you want me to tell you what I really want?" He nodded, not speaking, and drew her close again. "I want a home of my own, to fix up and take care of, and a husband to love and look after…and babies."

Dal laughed. "All at once?" Then he grew sober. "Cara, these days women have so many opportunities, so many career choices, it seems a shame for you to settle for—"

"Don't you see? For me, that's not settling, it's reaching!"

Her impassioned words obviously touched him. "But you need to go to college, to prepare yourself for life."

"Not everybody is suited for college,' Cara said quietly, firmly. "Dal, I'm good at my job."

"I know you are."

"And you can't tell me it's not one that's needed."

"No, of course not."

"I love what I do, and if you want to know the truth,

I kind of resent it when people consider it just a steppingstone to something better."

"Cara, I didn't mean to imply that your job isn't important. After what I've seen, I'd be the last one to say that. You work wonders with all your people, and it's no wonder they love you for it. But you need to make sure the choices you make now are the right ones. I don't want you to regret not going to college." His hands were on her shoulders now, and he held her at arm's length.

"If I want to, I can go later on. Women in their forties and fifties, and even older I'm sure, are going back to college, maybe even for the first time." She was quiet for a moment or two, then said slowly, "You sound as though you might…be around in my life, later on."

His voice was as low as hers. "I've thought about it."

"In spite of yourself."

"Cara, I'm not going to lie to you. My idea of the woman I wanted for a wife was not—"

"Not like me." Cara tried hard to keep the hurt from the words, but she wasn't entirely successful.

"I've hurt you. I'm sorry." He pulled her close. "It's just that you…you're different."

She wanted to ask if she were different from Janet Moody. If he didn't bring her name up now, then she couldn't mean all that much to him, could she? Cara slid her hands slowly up his chest, paused for a moment at his shoulders, then placed them on either side of his smooth-shaven face. "Dal, I've never felt this way about anyone before, so I don't know if it's love, or if it's what I've been looking for. But it doesn't seem bad; it seems good…." She pulled his head slowly down and stood on tiptoe to meet his lips. They were cool, from the wind, but they soon were warm, and at that particular moment nothing else mattered. They could work it out. She knew they could.

Chapter Eleven

The residents of Tillicum, including a secretly excited
Cara, watched the storm that began the evening of the
talent show gather in intensity. Cara's excitement
stemmed from the fact that she'd never been at the
beach during a really violent storm and had always
wanted to be. And though she was discreet most of the
time, it burbled out when she reached Virgil's.

She was blithely working her way through the accu-
mulated clutter in the kitchen. Though she'd stopped
several times to admire the brooding sky over the rest-
less, churning waters of the Pacific, she was almost finished. "Oh, Virgil, they say the winds might reach gale
force by tonight!"

He scowled. "You sound as though you might be
looking forward to it."

Cara eyed Virgil as she stood at the sink, holding a
dish towel and wearing a drapy, sexy-looking World War
II vintage dress with awesome shoulder pads. It *was*
brown, she'd reasoned, and matched her eyes; it *had*
been free and was part of the small but fairly interesting
new wardrobe from Mary and a few of her friends.
"Well, if we're going to have a storm anyway, and
there's absolutely nothing I can do about it, what's
wrong with enjoying it?"

Virgil's scowl deepened. "I don't know for sure, but

it can't be right." He sat at the table, his breathing clearly audible even though he tried hard to minimize it. His color was not good at all.

Cara dropped the dish towel and came over to him. "Virgil, the pain is worse, isn't it?"

"It's not so bad." But the blue tinge to his knuckles, the white lines around his mouth, showed the strain his body was suffering.

"Have you talked to Dr. Zylius lately?"

Virgil snorted. "There's nothing he can do—nothing anyone can do."

Ignoring the fact that she'd always tried hard to respect his natural reticence, Cara smoothed the gray hair back from his brow and combed it into place with her fingers. "You do have something to take when the pain gets really bad, don't you?" she asked softly.

He nodded. "I just took one. But it doesn't—" He stopped, then dragged the words out. "It doesn't always work like it's supposed to."

Cara's eyes were closed, her hand was warm and firm on the old man's shoulder now. *Oh, dear Lord, help my friend. Help him bear the pain. Take it from him...* The moments ticked away. Neither the old man nor the young woman spoke. His breath gradually slowed and became less raspy.

Finally he said, "Honey, you can't ever know how much it's meant to have you coming by to help out. Just your being here makes me feel better."

She tried to be casual as she scanned his face. He did look better. *Thank You.* The silent prayer resounded in her heart. She went to the stove to heat water for coffee. Aware that she needed to say something innocuous, something to make them both feel more normal, she announced brightly, "Dal said he'd be by for coffee around two. And as for how much it means for me to be here, well, it ought to be obvious how much I like doing it."

"Dal's coming by, is he?" Virgil's expression was ela-

142

borately casual now. "Tell you what, instead of me trying to be sneaky, how about if I just ask right out? How're you two getting on?"

Cara appeared to be concentrating on making coffee, but she couldn't control the soft and dreamy look that came into her eyes. "Virgil, I think I'm in love."

He let out a gusty sigh and nodded. "You'll pardon me if I don't act surprised. How about Dal?"

She stood with her back to the windows. The blue-gray of the lowering sky made a backdrop to her bright hair. "Oh, you know Dal. He probably never rushed into anything in his life."

"Hmph. I see you're getting to know him."

"I want to so much, Virgil. He's..." She trailed off.

Virgil whistled. "You do have it bad. He'll come around. I know it."

"That's sort of what Seretha said," Cara told him, remembering how she'd predicted Dal would ask her out.

"Seretha? That poor woman whose house burned?" When Cara nodded, he said, "Cara-Honey, I want to show you something." He went into the bedroom adjoining the kitchen, and she heard him rummaging around. When he returned, he had a long tin box in one hand and an envelope in the other. "This here's my will. It leaves everything to Dal since I never had children of my own. Now what I've been thinking on doing is having your name put on it, too."

Cara stared at him in wordless surprise.

"Why not? You want to live where you can see the ocean, don't you?"

"Yes, but—"

"You like this house. I know you do. And I swear it never felt like a real home till you started coming. You wouldn't mind living in it with Dal, I suppose."

"I..." She wanted very badly to say yes, but something held her back.

"It's settled. I'm going to make you my heir just like Dal is."

"Virgil, you have to remember, I'm just the woman who cleans your house!"

Virgil looked her straight in the eye. "It's right, this thing between you two. I never did feel good about that other woman."

Cara couldn't keep from asking, "Why not?"

"Um…she was awfully religious," he said, a frown lowering his brows.

"And that's bad?"

"Sometimes it seems to be a different thing than being Christian, but what do *I* know?" He shrugged. "Dal never talked much about her to me. It was always his mama—that's my sister—who felt like she had to give me bulletins."

Before she could stop herself Cara said, "He has a picture of her in his room."

"Why not? They grew up together. But I don't want to talk about Janet Moody. I want to talk about you and this house."

"But you can't just—"

He held up a hand. "Don't try to talk me out of it. My mind's made up. I want what I've got to belong to you both, legally. It'd make me rest easier."

"Virgil, I don't deserve it."

Fiercely he said, "We don't love people because they deserve it, girl. We just love 'em."

Cara swallowed. "I don't know what to say."

"There's something you can do to thank me." As the fierceness left him, his face grew wistful.

"Anything."

"You can sing at my funeral."

"Virgil!"

"I mean it. And I want you to sing something lively, something happy. Let's see." His eyes narrowed as he thought. "How about 'When the Saints Go Marching In'?"

Cara grinned, and it was real. "Sounds like a plan."

"Promise?"

"I promise." Cara thought regretfully of Seretha. She'd promised to take care of her house. *Well*, she vowed to herself, *nothing will make me break this promise to Virgil.*

"Good enough. Now let's not talk any more about all this. I'll tell Dal—say, I think that's him driving up now."

Cara ran to the window and saw that Virgil was right. Dal was just getting out of his car, and her heart did silly things at the sight of him. He wore his uniform, and she thought how fine he looked in the close-cut trousers and jacket. Of course, the hat wasn't what she'd have chosen, but on him even that looked good. She got out three clean mugs, but Virgil said, "None for me, Honey. I'm going for a little walk. Need to see what the tide brought up this time. Tell Dal I'll be back in a bit."

Before she could protest, he shrugged into his jacket and went out the back door, just as Dal came in the front.

"Virgil?" Dal called out.

Cara went as far as the door in the living room and stopped, a fit of shyness attacking her. "He went out, Dal." Cara saw now that he seemed preoccupied, even distant, a disappointment after last night's closeness. "He said he wanted to see what the tide brought in."

"How is he today?"

"He...he's in a lot of pain, I'm afraid."

Dal went to look out the window. He spotted Virgil walking slowly down the beach, stopping occasionally to stoop and examine something. "There has to be something more we can do for him."

The desperate, angry pain in his tone hurt Cara. "I asked Dr. Zylius, and he said there's nothing—short of a heart transplant, anyway."

He turned, his face set. "And he's too old, too sick to survive that, even if he wanted it."

"Which he doesn't. Dal, we're going to have to face it. He doesn't have long."

"That's easy for you to say."

145

"You're not being fair. You know I love him, too!"

Instantly his expression was contrite. "Of course you do. That was thoughtless of me, and I'm sorry. It's just that I'm worried about him, and I feel so helpless, so frustrated."

"I know. And you've got the storm on your mind, too." Cara knew what she said was true, and it took most of the sting away. "Do they feel it's going to get really bad?"

His face was grim now. "It could be the worst we've had in a long time."

Cara picked up the mug and started to pour him some coffee, but he shook his head. "None for me."

"But I thought that's why you came by, for coffee."

He covered the distance between them in a couple of strides and caught her close. He kissed her once, quick and hard, then said, "No. I came by to kiss you."

"Dal!"

A small smile touched his mouth as he drew away slightly. "Believe it. I also wanted to tell you that they're setting up quarters in the high school gym for people who really shouldn't stay in their own homes, particularly those that are more vulnerable."

"Like this one." Cara's brown eyes were wide.

"Right. I'll go out and talk to him. By the way, my mother is coming in from Arizona this afternoon."

"She is?"

Cara's dismay wasn't lost on Dal. He put his hand on her shoulder and squeezed gently. "Don't worry. She doesn't bite."

"I'm looking forward to meeting her." Cara wondered what Dal had told his mother about her, if anything.

"Would you go along with me to pick up some of the others, later this afternoon?"

"Of course. I'm through here." Her mind was going down the list, those she knew who shouldn't be alone

146

when the full fury of the storm hit. "What time do they say it'll be at its worst?"

"Sometime tonight." All business now except for the look in his eyes, he added, "I'll pick you up at your place in a couple of hours. And dress warmly. It's getting cold out." He didn't come over to her, or kiss her again, but she felt warmed by his steady gaze.

"I'll be ready," she said softly as he went out to find Virgil.

Cara had plenty to do before Dal was to pick her up, but her mind was not on what her hands were efficiently doing. As she tucked her toothbrush and a few cosmetics into her bag, she made herself face the fact that it was highly unlikely that Dal's mother would approve of her, much less like her. She stood in front of her closet, staring at the meagre contents, and realized there was nothing there which even faintly resembled an appropriate outfit in which to meet the awesome Mrs. Ross.

Suddenly she made a decision that was against her better judgment, but she knew she had to do it, even after a quick inventory of her funds. Forty-five minutes later, she walked out of one of Tillicum's few clothing stores dressed in a sedate navy wool crew neck sweater over a navy gingham button-down shirt, both neatly paired with an absolutely proper buff corduroy skirt. She also came out with very little money.

But when Dal came to pick her up, the surprised, approving look in his eyes made it almost worth it. "Mother's in the car," he said as he helped her into her coat, sneaking a quick kiss to her cheek.

Cara busied herself locking the door for two reasons: so he wouldn't remind her; and to hide her anxiety.

Whatever she'd expected, Mrs. Ross wasn't it. A tall, slim lady with hair the same color as Virgil's, she sat in the front seat. She smiled at Cara, but didn't move over, so Dal helped Cara into the back.

147

"This is Cara Morgan, Mother," he said as he got in. "She's been helping Uncle Virgil and a lot of the older ones around town."

"How do you do?" Mrs. Ross's words weren't cool, just proper.

At least that's what Cara told herself as she said a shade too brightly, "Hi! Isn't this storm something else? I've never been through a really bad one, and I'm excited." She knew she'd said the wrong thing as soon as Mrs. Ross spoke.

"You'd feel different if your home or your life were threatened, I'm sure," she said, not unkindly, but Cara felt chastened all the same.

"I...yes, you're right, of course," murmured Cara. She stared out at the driving, slanting rain, thinking that the woman would never approve of her, no matter what she said...or wore.

Mrs. Ross, her own smile bright, said, "I got a letter from Janet last week, son. When's the last time you heard from her?" When Dal answered that he'd gotten one last week as well, she said, "Oh, then you know she's coming home a little early?"

Dal slowed the car. The water now covered the street, making it look as though they were in a creek bed instead of two blocks from the school. As he turned the corner, making the water fan up, he said, "It's not really early, Mother."

"That's right, I suppose." She turned to face Cara now, still smiling. "It does take a long time to plan a wedding, especially when you've been away for two whole years."

A wedding. The only thing Cara could say was, "It does take a long time." She knew Mrs. Ross had brought up the subject deliberately, because she was in the car.

Dal said nothing as he braked in front of the gym, then got out and opened the umbrella for his mother. "Be back in a minute, Cara."

Mrs. Ross, who hadn't stopped smiling, said, "It's so

mind. But it was there all the same, like a spectre, waiting for her.

At Ladell Abernethy's she and Dal faced a crisis of sorts. The old woman steadfastly refused to leave Miss Scarlett behind. With the slit-eyed cat held close, its head sticking out of her heavy winter coat, Miss Abernethy declared, "I won't go if she can't!"

Though Dal looked as though he might refuse to take the creature, he surprised them both. "Of course you can take the cat, Miss Abernethy. But you have to come with us immediately. There's no time to waste, because we have a great many others to pick up."

Still suspicious, but not able to deny the fearsome sound of the wind outside shaking the small mobile home with ever-increasing force, Miss Abernethy inclined her head slightly in assent and even allowed Cara to put her arm around her as they slipped out the door. "Hold on to Scarlett, Miss Abernethy." Cara's words were snatched away by the wind. Dal walked protectively behind them as they fought their way to the car, their heads bowed against the onslaught of wind and rain.

Once they were safely inside the car, Cara said, her voice subdued, "It's worse than I thought."

Dal glanced at her as he started the engine and turned the heater up high. "We haven't seen the worst yet." Miss Abernethy's head was held as high as ever, but her chin shook slightly.

Glad that Dal hadn't actually chastised her again for her earlier excitement about the storm, Cara stroked the wide-eyed cat's damp head.

Before they reached the gym again the car was filled to capacity, with people as damp and wide-eyed as Miss Scarlett. Dal and Cara got them all inside the welcome warmth of the huge, well-lighted structure, and they all seemed to feel better except for Dal—as they were handed hot drinks.

He stood to the side, nursing his coffee mug, a

thoughtful, worried look on his face. Cara, having gotten her charges settled, came over to him. "You're thinking about Virgil, aren't you."

He nodded. "I'm going after him now, and I won't take no for an answer this time."

"Want me to go with you?" Cara glanced over to where she knew his mother was sitting. As she'd expected, the woman was watching her and Dal.

"No, you're needed here."

"Tell him I—" She started to say she loved him, but changed her mind. "Tell him to get over here right away, because I need moral support!"

"Don't worry. I'll get him here." He handed her his mug, and their hands touched briefly. Dal's eyes seemed to darken. He seemed about to say something more. Instead he put his sodden hat back on and walked away.

Cara watched him go, her heart longing for him to come back, for him to say...what? She sighed as he disappeared. Then she turned back to the noisy, crowded room. He was right about one thing. She was needed here. She looked around, trying to decide whom to speak to first as she smiled and waved to a woman in the makeshift "kitchen" set up in the far corner. "Miss Scarlett and Miss Abernethy first," she murmured to herself with a wry smile.

Because she got out so seldom—never was closer to the truth—Miss Abernethy, holding Miss Scarlett in her lap, was the center of attention. She was also reluctantly enjoying it very much. The cat, smoothing her damp fur with a rough, relentless tongue, barely acknowledged Cara, and neither did her new mistress. Miss Abernethy waved Cara away, not missing a word of some grievance she was relating with a relish to her audience. Cara smiled and moved on to where Mary sat.

Tom was bending over her, and as Cara approached, he straightened. His blue eyes lit at the sight of her. Then he glanced over to where Miss Abernethy was holding court. "Takes a hurricane to make some folks social. And that cat you gave her has done wonders."

"Would you believe she *took* her? I intended to ask you and Mary if you wanted her." Cara saw that the shadows beneath Mary's eyes were darker than usual. "Are you all right, Mary?" She knelt beside the wheelchair.

"I'm going to get her some soup." Tom reached for Mary's hand and clasped it tightly, the expression on his face clearly worried. "See if you can talk some sense into her." He turned and strode away before Cara could ask what he meant.

"Mary," she said softly, "what was Tom talking about?"

Mary's hands clutched the blue afghan tucked around her legs, and her face was set, rigid. It was a while before she said, each word ground out with effort, "We…I went to the doctor this morning. For an evaluation."

"And?"

Mary's face twisted. "It may be a very long time before I can walk the way…the way I used to, if I ever do at all."

"The therapy isn't working as well as you'd hoped." Cara's words were full of shared pain. "Oh, Mary, you've come so far."

"Not far enough," she said bitterly. "And I told Tom I don't want the celebration at all, ever!"

"You didn't!"

Anger lit Mary's blue eyes. "You don't think I have the right not to make a spectacle of myself? How would that look, the twisted old bride going down the aisle in a wheel chair?" Her voice had risen in anguish.

Cara was rubbing Mary's cold hands with her own warm ones. "In the first place, who says you have to go down the aisle?" She giggled, knowing it wasn't the thing to do, but a thought had just struck her. "Hey, Mary, times are different now. Who's to say you can't

153

have Tom come down the aisle to you this time?"

The idea struck Mary funny, too, for her face softened in a slight smile. "Cara, you always make me feel better. But—"

"No, wait. Before you refuse, think about it. You could be at the front of the church, standing up if you felt up to it, or enthroned in a beautiful chair if you wanted! It'd be great. You could plan a whole new scenario!" Cara's expression was excited as she warmed to her subject.

Mary stared at her, her own expression one of mingled love and exasperated resistance. When Cara finally stopped to take a breath, she said, "Cara, don't you think my feelings matter at all?"

The quiet words hit Cara hard. "Oh, Mary, of course they do. I'm sorry if you think I'm being insensitive."

"I don't think that at all, but I'm just not sure you or anybody, even Tom, know how much being like this affects me."

The contact of her hands and Mary's was still unbroken, and Cara felt as though the two of them were somehow isolated, almost encapsulated, in the noisy confusion of the crowd around them. "Of course you're right, none of us can really understand."

"Not even Tom…"

"Maybe especially Tom. He probably would much rather deny the whole thing. I imagine it's awfully hard for him to admit your…incapacity." She watched as Tom, mugs in hand stopped here and there to speak to someone on his way back to Mary.

"You seem to understand, Cara, at least a little."

"A little. That's usually all most of us can do when we're faced with another person's pain, understand a little. And Mary—"

"Go ahead and say it, whatever it is. I know you well enough to trust your instincts."

"I was just going to say that when it seems as though

I may be…pushing you, it's only because I can see both sides."

"And?"

Cara took a deep breath and plunged in. "Mary, Tom gives a hundred percent, and he deserves the same—even if you think you don't deserve him. When someone loves you like Tom does, it's insulting not to take it graciously and gladly. To love him the same way in return is the only thing worth enough to give back!"

Mary stared at her young friend. The intense, earnest appeal of Cara's words had pierced the shell of self-pity at last. It showed on her face. "Cara, I—" Tom came up just then, and she stopped and smiled tearfully up at him. "Oh, Tom…thank you!"

"For what? It's only coffee, and weak stuff at that. The soup's still not ready. Cara, you take this one, and I'll go back for mine."

Cara shook her head, believing very strongly that the two of them had some talking to do. "Thanks, I'll get my own, Tom. There's probably someone who wants to put me to work, anyway."

"I meant to ask earlier," said Tom, taking a sip of the hot coffee, "where's Dal?"

"He went to get Virgil." Not willing to place the burden of concern for Virgil on them, Cara hugged Mary once and whispered, "Remember, I love you," then moved off into the milling crowd. They felt like her own people. And that thought brought Seretha to her mind. She had to ask four people, but finally found one who knew where the phone was.

Though the call was necessarily short, because the lines had to be left open for emergencies, it was very satisfying. She found herself chuckling at Seretha's words. "I don't have much time, Cara dear. They're waiting for me." When Cara asked who, Seretha said, "My friends, dear, my friends!" Friends. If Seretha already had people she considered friends, she was going to be all right.

The smile Cara flashed at Mrs. Ross as she passed was fairly genuine. She understood Dal much better since she'd met his mother. Pushing aside the niggling anxiety she felt at the thought of Dal out in the storm looking for Virgil, Cara was finally about to get to the coffee, when suddenly the room was plunged into total darkness.

Though there were several gasps of horrified surprise, the main reaction was stunned silence, and what had been obscured by the chatter and activity of perhaps eighty people was now painfully apparent. Somehow the blackness intensified the sound of the storm's rage, and the collective fear in the gym made a funny taste in Cara's mouth. The wind was keening and howling as though it were a living creature bent on clawing its way in to them.

Cara swallowed her fear. She called out loudly into the black void, "Has anybody been to Carlsbad Caverns besides me?" A few half-hearted admissions were heard, but the oppressive silence inside the gym and the storm outside were about to claim them all.

"Do you remember how they turned out the lights and everyone sang 'Rock of Ages'?" Not waiting for them to answer this time, Cara's strong, husky voice began,

"Rock of Ages, cleft for me,
Let me hide myself in Thee...."

One by one the others joined her, until the music swelled and blotted out the awesome sound of the wind. Cara led them through it twice more. When the last note died away, the underlying fear was dispelled from the quiet. But the hush was still a waiting, anticipatory thing.

Almost of their own volition, Cara's hands began to clap. As if hypnotized by the darkness and by the sound of the clapping, the others once again joined in the

156

rhythm. "Step on the rock...." Cara sang the rollicking, happy chorus once through, and before she finished it a second time, several had caught on. Once through again and the whole gym was rocking to the tune of "Step on the Rock" and clapping hands. Working her way through a lifetime of choruses and scripture songs and old hymns, Cara and the others sang as if their lives depended upon it.

When the lights came on suddenly and Cara saw that Dal was standing to her left, she went to him and caught his arm, as glad to see him as she was that the lights were on again. She couldn't bring the words out, though, because suddenly a delayed reaction to the whole situation made her throat tight. But she clung tightly to his arm.

As the crowd began to mill around again, some of them still casting apprehensive glances at the rows of bright lights above, Dal drew her aside. "You were terrific."

Cara gazed up into his eyes, her relief stripping her of all the defenses she needed to keep herself cool in his presence. "When did you get back?"

"In time to see you prevent what could have been a potentially fatal situation." When he saw she was about to protest, he held up a restraining hand. "It's true. If this bunch had panicked in the dark, some of the older ones or the children might have been trampled. You were wonderful."

"I...thank you," she whispered. Then she remembered why he'd gone out again, why he was dripping wet. "Virgil, where is he?"

His face grew bleak. "I couldn't find him. His house is battened down, as though he prepared it for the storm. But there was no sign of him." Something must have caught his eye just then, because he moved slightly away.

"We'll find him," said Cara, wanting desperately to believe her own words.

"I'd better go and tell my mother. I know she's waiting to hear. She was just waving to me." He looked down at Cara. "Come with me?"

She shook her head. There were a couple of reasons why she was reluctant to go with Dal. She gave the lesser one aloud. "You go ahead. I'm sure they need me in the kitchen." The other reason—that she felt acutely uncomfortable around Dal's mother—was better left unsaid. The important thing was finding Virgil. She longed to put her arms around Dal at that moment and comfort him, reassure him. Instead, with her feelings showing in her wide brown eyes, she said softly, intensely, "You'll find him."

For a moment she was sure that the longing she felt was mirrored in his eyes. Then he nodded briefly and went to speak with his mother.

Chapter Twelve

The storm, at least the worst of it, was over by first light the next morning. All those who'd taken refuge in the gym had gone home, but the chaos created by their stay still had to be cleaned up and the building readied for the school day. Cara was exhausted, as was everyone else, but the fatigue of her body was nothing compared to the anguish of spirit when the news broadcast told of the finding of Virgil Penhollow's body.

Before that, everyone had been working together with an easy camaraderie, with shouts and jokes and lively music from the radio bouncing off the high ceiling. The clean-up crew was shooting baskets. But for the past half hour the few people who'd remained to help spoke in subdued tones. The most popular idea about Virgil's drowning—that he'd deliberately gone out in the storm with the intention of not coming back—provoked Cara to such anger that she clammed up after her initial horrified outburst and kept her distance from the others. Her passionate denial that Virgil would do such a thing apparently wasn't as interesting as speculating about suicide.

As soon as she could, Cara left, and because she'd ridden with Dal and her car was at the apartment, she walked the half mile to the beach access road. With a heavy heart, she made her way to the water's edge.

This morning the sea was almost docile, the waves decorously swelling far out, the shore swept clean by the high tides of the evening before. The sky wasn't blue. It was a high, clear gray. She walked, shoulders hunched against the cold wind, down the beach toward Virgil's house, and the tears that slowly coursed down her cheeks were so warm she hardly noticed them.

She kept trying to tell herself that he was in no more pain, that there would be no more fear of any kind. But she would miss him so. Not until she had climbed the rocky steps that led to his house, not until she had stood on the wide porch for a very long time looking out at the ocean and sky, did the tears stop and her chest loosen enough for her to breathe deeply again.

"Oh, Lord," she whispered, her hands gripping the weathered porch railing, "thank You for the assurance that Virgil is with You...." Eyes staring yet not seeing, she had an awesome thought. *There are millions of people who lose loved ones all the time, and they have no such assurance. I couldn't stand that....*Not to know, not to be secure in God's love seemed the most terrible thing imaginable.

Cara was so lost in her thoughts that she didn't hear Dal come up behind her. But when he put his hands on her shoulders and turned her to face him, she went without hesitation into his arms. Not even trying to stop the tears that began to flow again, Cara clung to him and he held her tightly. When the tears were finally spent, she raised her head to see that his own cheeks were wet. With gentle fingers she reached to wipe them away. "He's all right now, you know. He's all right."

"I've been trying to tell myself that."

"It's true. And he wouldn't want us to cry *too* long!" She laughed shakily.

Dal released her, his eyes going to the house. "There's something else he wouldn't have wanted."

"What, Dal?" asked Cara, knowing it would do him good to speak of his uncle, not to keep his feelings bottled up, which she suspected he usually did.

"He wouldn't want his house to stand empty."

"You're right. He would want you to be here."

"Not me, Cara, you."

His quiet words took her completely by surprise. "You can't mean you think I ought to move into the house now?"

"I certainly do, and as soon as you feel comfortable about it."

"I'm not sure I ever would unless—"

"Unless what? Didn't he tell you he was going to change his will and give you the house?"

"Yes, but…" Cara didn't finish. She couldn't tell Dal that what Virgil wanted was for the house to belong to both of them.

"It's the only sensible thing. You hate your apartment, which you can't afford, anyway. And Virgil wanted you here. He told me so."

"He did?" Cara asked softly. "When?"

"Yesterday, when I left you to go to find him. He told me the house had never had such love and care since he built it fifty years ago, that you'd made it a real home." He slammed a fist against the railing. "If only I'd forced him to come with me then!"

"Virgil wasn't the kind of man you could force, Dal," said Cara, troubled at his sudden vehemence. "If he wanted to stay, it was his decision."

"And I suppose you think he had the right to…to give up his own life, to stay out on the beach in a raging storm until—"

"Dal! You aren't like the others, surely you don't believe he committed—"

"Suicide." Dal furnished the harsh word, then said bitterly, "It's not confirmed, of course, and I think we'll be able to keep it off the death certificate. But the general consensus—of the coroner, and everyone down at the office—is that he knew exactly what he was doing, that he didn't want to face dying of heart failure."

"That's just not true!"

"You'll have to admit you didn't know him as well as the rest of us."

"I must have, because I know it was an accident," Cara said, her voice low and steady. "If you'll just let me explain—"

He cut her off, but not harshly now. "Not now, Cara, there's a lot to be done. I have to help my mother with the funeral arrangements and explain why you'll be living here in this house."

"I'm *not* going to be living here!"

His flinty gray eyes held hers. "Aren't you short of money?" She nodded, but before she could speak he went on. "And you hate the apartment, and you love Virgil's house. And he wanted you here. Can you deny that?"

"No, but—"

"I want you here." Suddenly he reached for her and pulled her almost roughly to him. He held her tight for a long time, not speaking. Then with the quiet, apologetic murmuring of the sea as a background, he said, "You will let me move you in as soon as possible, won't you?"

Cara felt dazed, but there was no real resistance in her heart. With different eyes she looked at the sturdy old house and knew how very much she would love living here—even more than she had at Seretha's. But she made one last effort. "Your mother, what will she say?"

"Don't worry, I'll make her understand. There's something else I have to make clear to her, but now is not the time. Later, when everything settles down after the funeral."

"The funeral." Cara thought suddenly what a heavy, sad word it was. She also thought of her promise to Virgil. She had not known how soon she would have to face it. "Dal, Virgil asked me to sing at his funeral. He told me exactly what he wanted, and I promised. Will you…can you arrange it for me?"

"Of course I will." He put his hand in his pocket and drew out a key. "This is to the back door. He has others hanging on the peg board in the kitchen, but I think you ought to have mine."

Still feeling as though too much had happened in too short a time, Cara said, "Do you realize this will be the fourth time in as many months that I've moved? That must be some kind of record." Her voice caught on the last word, but she had shed enough tears. *No more,* she promised herself, *at least not where anyone can see.*

"This time you can plan on staying."

"I'd like to stay somewhere." She could tell he was ready to leave, he was like a bird poised and ready for flight. "Don't worry about Virgil's things. I'll see that they're all packed and labeled, so your mother won't have to."

"She'll appreciate that."

Cara wasn't so sure that Dal's mother would appreciate anything she did. "Will I see you later?"

"There's going to be a lot to do, with the arrangements for the funeral and cleanup after the storm."

"You'll be busy, of course." Once again Cara had the feeling that he was holding her at arm's length. Except for that one brief time he'd held her, there had been no touch of any kind.

"Not too busy to move your stuff from the apartment when you get ready. By the way, the furniture stays here, all of it."

She knew from his tone there was no use arguing. "I'll take good care of it."

He nodded, and the look in his eyes could have meant several things. "I'll be in touch."

"Dal…" She hesitated. There was so much she wanted to say.

"Yes?" he said as he turned to go.

"Tell your mother how sorry I am."

"I will." Dal came over to her and brushed his lips

across her forehead, and then he left.

Cara heaved a huge, unladylike sigh of frustration, then went to let herself into her new home.

Having decided Dal was rushing things when he insisted she move in right away, Cara steadfastly refused to do so until after the funeral, which was set for two days later. Going through Virgil's things was a bittersweet experience for Cara. For someone his age Virgil had surprisingly few possessions. The house was sparsely furnished, but somehow Cara had always thought that added to its charm.

It was his personal belongings that made the wretched tears start. His clothes didn't even include a pair of slacks or a dress shirt, much less a suit. There were only dungarees and chambray shirts, the rough boots and jackets of a fisherman, and a trio of Navy watch caps. They had to buy him a suit to be buried in. Two small boxes held all his things, at least the ones Cara was willing to part with. The others—the fine collection of glass floats, the treasures which the sea had offered and Virgil had accepted—seemed to belong to the house.

The morning of the funeral Cara declared herself through with her housecleaning. She locked the door and while driving slowly back to her apartment to dress for the services, she had a most curious, disturbing sense of anxiety. As usual, she found herself praying aloud in the car.

"Lord, I don't know what's wrong with me! I do know Virgil's with You, and I'm really glad to have the chance to move into such a wonderful house, and I know it's what Virgil wanted and Dal seems to, too, but...."

She sighed as the light at the downtown intersection turned red. "But Dal seems so distant, and his mother doesn't seem to like me, and after today she probably never will." The light changed and Cara turned left, to-

164

ward the apartment building. She'd hardly seen Dal during the past couple of days, and they lived down the hall from each other. What would it be like when she lived in Virgil's house?

"Dear God, I know I asked for a man to love, to share my life with, and I know Dal suits me. But it's not working out like I thought it would. Please, give me some peace. Help me not to be so…so agitated….Lord, settle my spirit…."

As Cara pulled into the parking area she saw Dal getting out of his car, and her breath caught in her throat. Then a sudden calm washed over her, like the waves of her beloved ocean caressing the shore on a calm day. "Thank You," she whispered, and got out, for Dal had seen her.

They walked inside together, Dal making small talk, Cara listening and not saying much. At his door he stopped, and his eyes went over her from the bandannaed head and blue overalls—a gift from Tom, this time—to her moccasined feet.

"How long will it take for you to get ready? You could ride over with me."

"Don't worry, I'll wear the dress you gave me to the funeral."

"I wasn't thinking—"

"Weren't you wondering if I'd wear the right thing?"

"Now is not the time to talk about this, Cara."

She started to ask when the time would be, but she saw the fatigue and the sorrow in his eyes and she regretted her thought. "You're right, of course. I'll be glad to go with you. How's your mother? I…I've got brothers, and they mean a lot to me."

He nodded, his gray eyes somber. "She's all right. They were never really close. He was kind of the maverick in the family."

"Like me." Before Dal could comment, she said, "Give me twenty minutes. And I promise you won't have any reason to be ashamed of me."

Dal didn't touch her, but his gaze was steady. "Did I ever say I was ashamed of you?"

"No, but—"

"You're a lovely woman, Cara, and any man would be proud to be seen with you." He gave her a little push. "Now go on and get dressed."

Cara did as she was told, and half an hour later they walked into the little church. "I have to check with the pianist, Dal," said Cara. She saw with a lurch in her stomach that the sanctuary was almost full. Dal nodded, and she moved away, knowing she was being watched with interest. Many of those present were familiar, because they were regulars at the Senior Center. Her smile was bright, but this was one time she definitely would have preferred to be in the background.

The young minister in charge was new in Tillicum, and had only met Virgil a few times. But he'd done his homework and had talked at length to people who knew Virgil well. And he spoke with confidence when he assured them that Virgil was safe with the Lord. Though Cara was paying close attention to his words, she was still caught off guard when he said, "And now, Miss Cara Morgan will sing, at Mr. Penhollow's request."

Cara stood up so suddenly that she almost fell. She caught herself just in time. A nervous little bubble of laughter squirmed around in her as she made her way to the side of the room and faced the congregation, both hands clutching the music stand. Her wide brown eyes scanned the waiting faces, and the first thing she said was totally unplanned; it just seemed to pop out. "Oh, don't you wish Virgil were here so he could see how many of us cared about him?" She smiled through the sudden tears that stung her eyes. "I miss him, and I know you do, too. I didn't know him as long as all of you, but he was very special to me...and I like to think I was to him, too." Cara saw a few nods and some answering smiles. They gave her courage.

"There's something I want to tell you about Virgil Penhollow." A hushed expectancy fell over the crowd. Everyone there was listening to Cara, especially Mrs. Ross, although her expression had a degree of apprehension mixed in it. "We—Virgil and I—talked about his feelings about death more than once. He was like most of us, afraid he wouldn't be able to face it with courage, that the pain would be more than he could bear honorably. And…" Cara hesitated, but she knew she had to say the next words no matter what anyone thought, whether what she was doing was proper or not. "Some people around town are saying that the way he died was a kind of suicide." A ripple of sound went around the room. "It isn't true."

Her eyes were drawn to Dal, to the question she read not only on his face, but on the face of Virgil's sister and most of the others in the room. They all wondered. "I know because we talked about it last week, and Virgil was absolutely convinced that God would give him special grace…dying grace, when he needed it. So you see, what happened to Virgil was an accident, but God used it. Virgil is with Him now. When he died, he was just doing what he'd always done, enjoying the sea. I know it," she finished simply, with absolute, undeniable assurance. Then very quietly she sang, without the piano, all the verses of "Amazing Grace."

The silence in the place was total, and when Cara began to sing "When the Saints Go Marching In," they sat with smiles on their faces, as if they were bemused. And just as they had in the gym on the night of the storm they began to sing with Cara. The pace was anything but slow and funereal. It was what Virgil had asked for, singing with joy. By the time they finished everyone was smiling outright.

Cara glanced over at the young minister, who bowed his head. His closing prayer was simple: "Oh, God, we know You have received unto Yourself the soul of Virgil Penhollow. May each of us remember him with the love his friend Cara has shown. Dear Lord, teach us to love and accept each other as we are....Amen."

There was a great deal of talk, of reminiscing about Virgil, and not all of it was quiet and subdued, either. Cara stood to one side, thinking the service was what he had wanted. Only when Mrs. Ross came toward her did she have that sinking feeling again, the feeling that no matter how much Virgil would have liked the service, Virgil's sister was going to roast Cara alive.

She couldn't have been more wrong. Mrs. Ross said, "Thank you, Cara. I can't imagine how you had the courage to do it, but I'm very grateful."

"You're grateful?"

"I am. Oh, there'll still be some who will talk and doubt that Virgil's death was accidental, because that's what they'd rather believe. I...I'll have to admit I wondered," she said, and Cara could see how hard it was for her to say the words.

"Mrs. Ross, your brother was a fine, courageous man. I was proud to have him as a friend, and I can't tell you how glad I am to have gotten to know him," Cara said softly.

Mrs. Ross was obviously struggling with her feelings. "You make me wish I hadn't wasted so much time, that I'd gone over to his place more often. You know how he never liked to leave home. I guess I got on my high horse and told him if he wanted to see me, he could come to my house once in a while. I was...stiff-necked about it...." She halted as a woman came up.

Cara could almost see the mask of polite correctness fall over Mrs. Ross's face as she said, "Oh, Jennie, I was just telling Miss Morgan how much we appreciate the fine job she's doing with our senior citizens, the wonderful things she did for Virgil."

Cara excused herself quietly as soon as she could manage it, thinking she would never, if she lived to be a hundred, learn the polite social games almost everyone seemed bound to play. And she was sure she didn't want to. Just as she was about to slip out the door, she felt a hand on her arm.

It was Dal. "If you'll remember, you came with me. Are you ready to leave?"

"Yes, but isn't there a graveside service?"

He shook his head. "Mother said no."

There was weak, filtered sunlight as they stepped outside and stood for a few moments on the steps of the church. "She probably figured that was all she could take after I got through." Cara began to walk toward the car, but she stopped. "I'm not being fair. She even came over and thanked me, and I know she meant it."

Dal's hand was at her back as he propelled her gently to the car and opened her door. "You seem to think she would disapprove regardless of what you do." Without waiting for an answer, he went around and got in, too. It wasn't until they reached Virgil's house a few minutes later that Cara spoke.

"Dal, there's so much I'm confused about."

"Like what?" He cut the engine and sat staring out at the ocean.

"Like, if I'm dressed right"—she glanced down at her neat, pretty dress, the proper shoes—"can I do whatever I want to, like sing lively songs at a funeral and tell everyone Virgil's death was an accident...and it be accepted? I'll bet if I'd had on something funky, and did what I just did, no one would have been able to take it. They would have been blinded by the way I looked."

"I don't understand what you're getting at, Cara," said Dal, his gray eyes on her now.

"Oh, I don't either! Okay, I'll try again. Is the way we dress more important than what we are inside, the real people we are?"

"No, of course it isn't, but—"

"Then why does everyone make such a fuss about it?"

Dal frowned a little. "If you'll let me finish, I'll try to tell you what I think."

169

"Sorry," said Cara, but not too meekly.

"It's all right. I'll have to admit I've thought a lot about this subject since I met you." He paused, then added thoughtfully, "I decided that one reason people dress a certain way is because it's expected of them."

"They conform," murmured Cara, as if being a conformist were synonymous with being a traitor.

"It's more than that, Cara. For instance, when I wear my uniform people know I represent the law, that they can expect certain things of me."

"I see. You mean if we see a nun in a habit, or a fireman all suited up, or a young woman in heels of the proper height and a dress the proper length, we make decisions about their character."

"I guess that's what I meant, but when you say it like that I'm not so sure," Dal said.

"And if you see a young woman in a crazy getup you immediately assume she's crazy...or on drugs." The words were out. She couldn't take them back.

"You're talking about yourself, of course." He took a deep breath and rubbed his temples as if his head hurt. "Cara, you know you've proved yourself over and over, that people see past the way you dress—"

"Exactly! They see past it."

"But you're forgetting something."

"What?"

"The very fact that you *do* have to prove yourself. Wouldn't it be better not to have to, not to have strikes against you from the very beginning of a relationship? Why not dress normally and avoid the problem?"

"What do you mean by that?" Her voice was low and angry.

"I mean that if you care whether or not others accept you, you might have to conform. If you don't care, just do as you please and go on about your business." His tone was dangerously close to anger too, now. "Are you packed? I have some time this evening, and we can get you moved into the house."

"I've changed my mind."

"You've *what?* Are you saying you don't want to move in?"

"I'm saying I don't want to live in your house!" She was staring out the window, her eyes brimming with tears. "Take me back to the apartment, please."

Throughout the short trip back to town, they both maintained a stony silence.

Cara got out as soon as he stopped the car, but before she could close the door he said, "This isn't what I want, Cara."

"Well, it's what *I* want!" she cried, and slamming the door much harder than she should have, she ran inside.

But it isn't what I want, either, she thought as she walked slowly down the dim hallway to her apartment, that awful, dreary apartment she hated. Worst of all, Cara didn't know what she did want.

Chapter Thirteen

In the weeks between Thanksgiving and Christmas Cara was busy, almost too busy, but she preferred it that way.

She and Mrs. Lane had come to an agreement on several things. Not only was Cara given two more clients, she was now officially the Assistant Activities Coordinator at the Senior Center. The woman in charge was only too happy to allow Cara free rein and had given her blessing to Cara's suggestion that they begin tryouts for an old-fashioned melodrama.

Everything would have been perfect if it hadn't been for the fact that, although she saw Dal at church and occasionally downtown or at the Senior Center, he was never more than polite. He never called or came by. Then, as the days melted into weeks, she decided that even if he were to call, she would hang up. A few days before Christmas the phone rang, and her resolution was put to the test.

"Cara, I was wondering if you're going to the Stewarts' anniversary party."

"I suppose so, since I've been running an average of three errands a day for them, helping to get things ready."

Dal couldn't have missed the sharp edge to her words. "You're still angry, aren't you."

"Of course not. Why should I be?"

"Come on, you don't seem like the kind of woman to stay mad."

"I'm not mad."

"Don't tell me that. I can feel the heat over the phone!"

She laughed in spite of herself. "Okay, I am mad! I kept thinking you'd call, or come by…and you didn't."

He paused, then said, "There were some things I had to take care of."

"What things?"

"Let me take you to the party and I'll tell you."

"That's bribery."

"You could call it that. How about it?"

"You sound different. Has something happened?"

"Is six o'clock early enough to pick you up?"

"Yes, but—"

"See you then."

Before she could protest again he hung up, leaving her scowling at the phone. But not for long. With a lighter heart than she'd had for weeks, she lost herself in the fun of getting ready for a date—with Dal. A long, hot soak in a scented tub, a careful shampoo and set, and…and… She grinned almost all the way through the twenty minutes it took to paint her positively decent fingernails a peachy pink.

When she had slipped on her new dress, she knew she could pass even Mrs. Ross's examination. It was a soft peach color, with a draped cowl neckline and long, tight sleeves. She had no jewelry on except for the tiny pearls she always wore in her ears, but when she looked in the mirror, she had the uncomfortable feeling someone else was staring back at her.

Dal's reaction helped a little. His eyes kept straying to her in the car, and at the Stewarts' celebration she caught him watching her several times during the evening. It was all she could do to keep her mind on what she was supposed to be doing. With satisfaction she thought of the arrangements Tom and Mary had decided on; the word *compromise* didn't quite fit.

At a few minutes before eight o'clock, Tom made his way to where Mary sat. She looked radiant in her white dress, with its train flared out artfully to one side. After a quick kiss on her brow, Tom sat in the chair beside hers.

One of Cara's jobs was to turn up the volume of the music so everyone would know something was about to happen. There were a great many people milling about, but when the sounds of the wedding march came flowing from the speakers, they quieted and turned to watch the couple.

Tom was dressed in a dark blue blazer and gray trousers, his navy tie knotted carefully against the white of his shirt. He and Mary were smiling at each other as though they were quite alone; they even seemed unaware of the minister who was walking slowly toward them. When he stopped about three feet away, they stood together, Tom's hand protectively under Mary's elbow. A few seconds later, the music stopped and the deep, pleasant voice of the pastor broke into the hush.

"We are gathered together in the sight of God and these assembled witnesses to rejoice with Tom and Mary, whose pledges to each other, given fifty years ago, are still precious and binding."

Cara's throat was tight as she stood watching on the far side of the room. She dared not look for Dal; she was afraid her feelings would show if her eyes met his. *Oh Lord,* she prayed, *this is what I want…a love that lasts, that is true and real, even when life is far from easy.…*

She knew how difficult it had been for Tom and Mary to work out a plan that was comfortable for them both. The important thing was that they'd cared enough to keep trying until they solved the problem. When the simple ceremony was over and Tom had bent to kiss Mary, Cara's eyes misted.

"I should have known you were the kind who cries at weddings, especially a rerun."

She jerked her head up to see Dal grinning down at her. "And I should have known you'd be the kind who'd poke fun!"

"Hey, let's don't get off on the wrong foot. This is a happy occasion, remember?"

"You remember it, too." Cara sniffed, glad she had a handkerchief.

"Cara, when can you leave? There are some things we need to talk about."

The crowd was beginning to move toward Tom and Mary, who had sat down again according to the plan. "Look at her, she's like a beautiful queen."

"You're avoiding my question. When can you leave?"

She made herself look up into his eyes and wouldn't let herself look away. "Dal, we're so different, and there's Janet—"

"Meet me at the front door in half an hour, all right?" His hand reached for hers and the simple contact made Cara shiver, but she nodded wordlessly. He gave her hand a squeeze, then joined the crowd who were waiting their turns to congratulate Tom and Mary.

Almost an hour later, Cara extended her hands to the bright blaze Dal had built in the fireplace of the snug stone house, which still had painful echoes of Virgil. Dal's plants and books and seascapes had changed the look of it a great deal, and when she made a comment to that effect Dal said, "I didn't bring you here to talk about the house."

She turned to face him. "Why did you bring me here?"

His gaze on her was thoughtful. "You've changed since I first came across you on the beach that evening."

"And are you pleased with the changes?"

"Very pleased." He came to stand close by her and took her hands in his. "Your hands look pretty. I knew

176

they would, once you let the nails grow. Almost as pretty as your feet," he teased.

"Dal, don't," she said, pulling away from him.

"Why not? I want you to know how much you please me."

She stared up into his gray eyes; they looked almost black in the firelight. "Sometimes I think I'm losing myself. When I look in the mirror, the reflection doesn't seem like me...."

"It's you, all right—the real you, the person I knew you could be. I was very proud of you tonight." His hands were on her shoulders now, caressing the silky smoothness of her dress.

"I'm just not sure about things anymore, Dal."

"Answer one question. Do you love me?"

"I..."

"Well, do you?"

"Yes, I can't help it. I do."

He laughed and caught her close. "Why should you want to help it?" His lips were warm and demanding, and Cara felt the heat of his body as he kissed her. When he had finally stopped, Dal said what she'd hoped to hear. "Cara, I love you. And I'm tired of living here alone. I want you here with me."

"Is that a proposition, or what?" She tried to make the words sound joking, but they snagged in her throat.

"You know me better than that."

"No, I don't, not really. But I want to." She put her forehead on his chest. "What about Janet?"

"Remember that day you told me you weren't used to having someone make love to you? The day of the storm?" Her head moved against his shirt. "I hadn't allowed myself to admit it, but that's what I was doing."

"And I wanted you to."

"It wasn't fair to you. That's when I made up my mind to write Janet and tell her about us."

"You wrote Janet about us?"

"Yes, and yesterday I got an answer."

"And?"

"She reminded me that we knew there was a good chance one of us would find someone else if we were separated for so long."

"That doesn't sound like the kind of love Tom and Mary have, the kind I want."

"It was never that way between Janet and me."

"Then why did your mother say that, about Janet coming home to plan your wedding?"

"A fair question." He let go of her and went to the fireplace. On one knee, he poked and jabbed at the glowing logs until they leaped into brightness again. He didn't turn to face her as he said, "I'm not proud to admit that it was convenient for me."

"Convenient? I think you'd better explain that!"

"I told you I wasn't proud of it. But the arrangement kept my mother happy, kept her from hounding me to find a woman and settle down. She likes Janet." His jaw clenched. "She didn't say it in so many words, but I think Janet felt the same way. If we were engaged she could say no with a clear conscience to men she didn't want to date."

"So you sort of used each other," Cara said thoughtfully. "And you used your relationship with her to protect yourself against me at first, didn't you?"

"That makes me sound…cold-blooded."

"Yes, it does, doesn't it?" she said in a small, tight voice. "There are a couple of other things I'd like to know. Have you told your mother about your plans for you and me?"

"No, I wanted to settle things between us first."

Cara certainly couldn't deny the wisdom of that, but the other question burned in her brain. "Why didn't you tell me you'd written to Janet? Why did you let me stew all this time?"

"I thought it was best to clear things with her before I approached you again, that's all."

"You never thought about how I might feel, being so…so separated from you?"

"I felt the same way," he said, his voice low.

"But you obviously didn't feel you could trust me."

"No, that isn't what I thought. Cara, you're not being fair."

"It isn't fair that you don't think of me as an equal, as someone you can share important decisions with," she said, angry and hurt at the same time. "Dal, why did you tell me you loved me *now?*"

"Because I do."

"You do now. But you didn't, or couldn't before."

"Before what?"

"Before I started trying to dress right and let my fingernails grow…Dal, you may think all of that made me different, but it didn't! Except…" His silence neither discouraged nor encouraged her. "Except that I'm no longer sure of myself. Is that what you want, for me to depend on you, have you pick out my clothes, change my bad habits?"

"Of course not. You're taking this wrong. I was trying to help you."

"Were you trying to help me when you took me shopping in Newport instead of here in Tillicum where your friends might have seen us, when you took me on a picnic on a deserted beach? Weren't you ashamed to be seen with me?" Cara was suddenly afraid, not certain she wanted to know the answers to her questions.

The look of guilt that flashed over his face was quickly gone, but it was undeniable. "Cara, that has nothing to do with the way I feel about you now."

"Doesn't it? Would you still want me if I stopped trying to dress to please you?"

"Do you intend to do that?"

"I just might!"

"Why, Cara? Have you ever thought seriously about why you dressed the way you did? And remember, it was you, not me, who brought this whole thing up."

179

"I'll remember, and yes, I do know why." Her eyes were flashing now, her color high. "I did it for two reasons. Because I like old things, and—"

"Wasn't it because you wanted to rebel, to show people you're above convention?"

"Is that what you think? That I'm just a kid who wants to thumb my nose at society?" His hard stare dared her to deny it. "It's just not true, Dal. You don't know me at all."

For the first time that evening, a look of uncertainty crossed his face. "If I've been wrong, I'm sorry."

"The main reason I started wearing second-hand clothes—besides the fact that I enjoyed them—was because they were cheap, and I didn't have much money. It seemed dumb to go into debt just to look like everyone else." Dal looked uncomfortable, but she went on relentlessly. "You, and other people, judged me because of those clothes. Well, I don't like that."

"You're placing more importance on this than you should."

"That's funny, or it would be if it weren't so backwards. I'm not the one who's putting the importance on it, you are! You make me feel that if I dress 'properly,' everybody will like me better…if I do, you'll love me…Dal, that's putting limits on your love!" Cara's voice sounded cold and lonely in the dim, firelit room. She went to the pegs by the door where her coat hung and shrugged into it. "I think it's time for me to go."

"Not until we get this straightened out." He strode over to her, but she backed away.

"Don't touch me again. You know what it does to me."

"And is that bad?"

"I…no, it's not, but I want—"

"What do you want?"

"I want a man who can accept me just the way I am, crazy clothes and chewed fingernails and all! Oh, Dal, that's the way I love *you*, just the way you are…." She

180

choked on the sob that rose in her throat. "Please take me home."

"Cara, don't—"

"Take me home, Dal."

He shrugged, but he said nothing more to persuade her to stay. At the door of her apartment, his gray eyes troubled, he did venture to say, "We're missing something here, but I'm not sure what it is."

She refused to look up; she was afraid she'd relent and throw herself into his arms. "Good night, Dal." She started to unlock her door and found to her intense embarrassment that she'd neglected to lock it—again. As she slipped inside she heard him say, "You're right, maybe you haven't changed so much after all." His footsteps sounded terribly loud as he walked away.

Mortified and mad in equal amounts, she sat on the ugly sofa and looked around the ugly room and couldn't hold back the tears. "This is going to be an awful Christmas...."

Cara did try, but not even the fact that her mother was fixing all of her favorite dishes for Christmas dinner nor the fact that Dr. Zylius had allowed Seretha to come home with her made her spirits rise.

They decorated the tree with the old ornaments that usually brought such pleasure to Cara, all the lovely family heirlooms, the homely things she and her brothers had made as children. Ben had let Cara choose the Noble fir, one of the most beautiful trees they'd ever had, even though he always insisted it was a man's job.

When Ben had put the angel on top and switched on the tiny, starry lights, Seretha clapped her hands like a child. "Oh, it's so wonderful of you to share your Christmas with me!"

A pang shot through Cara. She thought of Seretha's son who hadn't, as far as she knew, come to see his mother in more than six months, not even when the house had burned. Cara suspected he might not come at all now, since there would be no inheritance other than the proceeds from the sale of the property where the burned house stood. She came out of her despondency just long enough to go to Seretha and hug her tightly.

After a miserable sleepless night, not even the Christmas morning ritual of opening gifts was enough to make Cara smile. Her father finally said, "For heaven's sake, gal, lighten up! Contrary to what some of those guys may have tried to make you believe, no man's worth ruining Christmas for."

To his dismay Cara burst into tears and ran upstairs to the sanctuary of her bedroom, refusing to come down even when her mother called that they had company, and a little while later, that dinner was ready.

"I'm not hungry, Mom. Go ahead without me!"

A moment later Lexie appeared at the door. "Cara, get up and wash your face and come downstairs. Your friend Dal is here, and dinner is ready."

"Dal? How long has he been here? Why didn't you tell me?"

"I just did, and he's been here long enough for your dad and him to have…a talk about you." She came over to where Cara was now sitting on the edge of the bed, panic-stricken. "We both like him, Honey, a lot. Now stop acting like a child and come downstairs."

"But…" Cara looked down at the demure white gown she was wearing, the gown that had been a topic of discussion between her and Dal on more than one occasion. She'd cinched it with a crimson leather cummerbund for Christmas. "I'd better change—"

"You look fine." Her mother met her eyes for a long moment, then Cara nodded as her mother said gently, "Just be yourself, and it'll be fine."

Downstairs she was able to smile when Dal looked up from a conversation with her father, and Seretha made a noise that sounded very much like a giggle. Her blue eyes were bright as she said, "I knew I was going to have a good dinner, but you didn't mention there'd be entertainment!"

The old woman's face was suddenly, solemnly innocent when Cara glared at her and then she said, "Dal, how nice of you to come."

His smile was grave. "It was nice of your mother to invite me to dinner when I called from Salem a while ago."

That dinner was up to her mother's usual standards, and everyone but Cara laughed a great deal during it. She was uncharacteristically quiet, and although she wanted to be cool and objective, she had to admit Dal had never looked better. He was dressed in a dark gray blazer and light gray slacks. Though he wasn't wearing a tie, his white shirt somehow gave the impression of formality.

He turned to Seretha. "Are you saying you don't mind going back to the Care Center?"

"No, Sheriff. In a way, I'm looking forward to it."

That brought Cara out of her self-imposed silence. "Really, Seretha?"

"Really. I don't know if I ever told you, but all my life I wanted to be a missionary." She made a little face. "But my husband, Neil, certainly had no such ambitions, so I put the idea aside."

Cara smiled at her friend. "You'd have been a great missionary."

"Would have been? Cara dear, every day that passes I'm more convinced that I am one now! Have you any idea how many people there are in that place who don't know the least true thing about God, how many of their relatives, and friends, don't either?" With a wry smile she added, "Not to mention some of the employees. It's the mission field I never got to, the chance to be a missionary I thought I'd lost forever."

"That's neat!"

"It is, isn't it? I thought I'd die at first, I hated it so much there. And I was angry that all my lovely things were gone. But after that day we sang the hymns, after you bought me that new Bible and I began to read again, people began to see something I'd almost thrown away with both hands...my faith."

Ben shook his head. "As Cara says, Mrs. Hodges, that's neat."

"He's right," put in Lexie warmly. "It's wonderful."

"It is, so don't let me catch any of you feeling sorry for me!" Seretha laughed and added, "Now, what's for dessert?"

"We've got three kinds of pie. Come take your pick," said Lexie, glancing at Ben. He was watching Dal thoughtfully and didn't see her wordless hint for him to come, too. "Ben, are you ready for dessert in the den with Seretha and me?" she asked pointedly.

"Oh, sure," he said and got up to follow her.

The big old dining room suddenly seemed very quiet. Cara picked at the food on her plate. She'd hardly been able to eat a bite. She didn't speak, didn't look at Dal. She was determined to leave things up to him. But when the seconds ticked by and still he didn't break the silence, she finally said, "Why did you come, Dal?"

"Because I couldn't stay away from you," he answered simply. "Since that evening I first saw you on the beach, no matter how hard I tried, I couldn't stay away."

"You tried hard, hm?" She glanced at him, saw the look in his eyes and the spurt of aggravation she felt melted away.

"I brought you a Christmas present."

"Oh, I don't have anything for you!"

"Still mad at me?"

"Not mad, just...just afraid I won't ever be the person you want me to be..." She couldn't help it. Her heart was in her eyes.

Abruptly he stood up. "Let's go for a walk."

She nodded. "Mom, Dad," she called, "Dal and I are going for a walk."

184

"We'll save you some pie," her mother called back.

"Don't count on it," Seretha said pertly to Dal.

At the door Cara took down her navy pea coat, and glanced at the white gown. "It might look sort of funny with this."

Dal helped her put the coat on. "You look beautiful, just the way you are."

Outside the air was cold and clear. There'd been no snow, but then, white Christmases in Salem are rare. They walked for perhaps half a mile without speaking, Cara's feet naturally following the path they'd taken all her life, until they stopped on a rise that gave a sweeping view of the gently rolling, still green countryside.

Finally Dal said, "Don't you want to see what I got you for Christmas?" He drew out a small square jeweler's box. "If it's not what you want, we'll get another one."

But when he slipped the ring on her finger, she shook her head, the diamond blurring through her tears. "I love it."

"And I love you, Cara." She swayed toward him, her eyes closed. The kiss wasn't long, but it brought a deep, satisfied sigh from them both. "You're the person I want right now. You've always been, but I was too stubborn to see it."

"Do you mean that?"

"I do. When I got to thinking of how you helped the Stewarts, and Seretha and Virgil...Cara, the list just kept getting longer—the style show, the talent show. And now, every place I go I hear about the melodrama."

"But those things are fun for me—"

"It goes beyond fun. That business in the gym during the storm, and Virgil's funeral—you make a difference in people's lives. How could a man not want a woman like you? I've been doing a lot of thinking and remembering. I realize that what you are is a lot more important than how you dress or," his fingers felt for hers,

185

"whether you bite your nails. You haven't started again."

His gentle stroking of her fingers made Cara shiver. "Dal, I ought not to bite my nails. Some of the other things you wanted...well, I need to think through them and decide for myself. Can you take me as I am now and hope for the best?"

"Yes, I can. Would you like to hear what I've decided about us?"

"More than anything in the world." She laid her head on his shoulder and slipped her arms around his waist beneath his jacket.

"You'd better watch that, or I might not be able to think."

"Try hard. I need to touch you, and besides, I'm cold."

He laughed and pulled her even closer. "The only explanation I can give you is that it was an answer to prayer, because the conclusions I came to are a lot different from the way I used to feel."

"Tell me."

"I decided it wasn't right for a man to set out deliberately to change the woman he loves. And if she loves him—"

"I do, I do!"

"Stop interrupting," he commanded, but he softened it with a kiss. "I decided that those two people will just naturally make different and better people of each other...if they allow it."

"That's beautiful."

"The thing I was leaving out was that I'm not perfect myself and...rather than try to change you, I should accept you."

"You say you're not perfect? I never thought of that!"

"Cara, be serious."

"I am. But now that you mention it, I can see you're right. You're *not* perfect." She laughed and hugged him tight.

186

He heard the tears in her laughter and felt them when he touched her cheeks. "I didn't mean to make you cry."

"I love you. And someday I'll be everything you want in a woman." Her face was buried in his damp jacket.

"You are now. Your father said—"

"You talked to my dad about me?" she asked as she came up for air.

"I even asked for your hand in marriage, Honey. It seemed the thing to do at the time." A little grin quirked his mouth.

"And what did he say?"

"That it was up to you, that he and your mother trust your judgment. Will you marry me, Cara?"

Her eyes sparkled with tears, but they were more than a little mischievous. "You know I will. Anything to get out of that awful apartment and into Virgil's house—"

Dal chuckled. "Our house, Honey…our home. It'll be what Virgil always wanted, a home." He kissed her wet cheeks, her eyes. "We'll grow together, change together."

She nodded, still close enough to brush his mouth with hers. "Oh, Dal, it's going to be so much fun!"

He laughed, too, now, and held her so tight it was difficult for either of them to breathe. "I think you're right again. You're what I need, someone to make things fun. Would you answer one more question?" She gazed up at him expectantly, adoringly. "Did your mother have any lemon meringue pie?"

"Let's go see!" She caught his hand. "I'll race you…"

Their laughter seemed to float up on the still, cold, Christmas day air, to follow them as they ran.

Promise Romances® are available at your local bookstore or may be ordered directly from the publisher by sending $2.25 for each book ordered plus 75¢ for postage and handling.

If you are interested in joining Promise Romance® Home Subscription Service, please check the appropriate box on the order form. We will be glad to send you more information and a copy of *The Love Letter,* the Promise Romance® newsletter.

Send to: Etta Wilson
Thomas Nelson Publishers
P.O. Box 141000
Nashville, TN 37214-1000

*OTHER PROMISE ROMANCES®
YOU WILL ENJOY*

$2.25 each

Dear Reader:

I am committed to bringing you the kind of romantic novels you want to read. Please fill out the brief questionnaire below so we will know what you like most in Promise Romances®.

Mail to: Etta Wilson
               Thomas Nelson Publishers
               P.O. Box 141000
               Nashville, Tenn. 37214-1000

1. Why did you buy this Promise Romance®?

☐ Author   ☐ Recommendation
☐ Back cover description   from others
☐ Christian story   ☐ Title
☐ Cover art   ☐ Other_____

2. What did you like best about this book?

☐ Heroine   ☐ Setting
☐ Hero   ☐ Story line
☐ Christian elements ☐ Secondary characters

3. Where did you buy this book?

☐ Christian bookstore ☐ General bookstore
☐ Supermarket   ☐ Home subscription
☐ Drugstore   ☐ Other (specify)_____

4. Are you interested in buying other Promise Romances®?

☐Very interested   ☐Somewhat interested
            ☐Not interested

5. Please indicate your age group.
   ☐Under 18   ☐25-34
   ☐18-24   ☐35-49   ☐Over 50

6. Comments or suggestions?

7. Would you like to receive a free copy of the Promise Romance® newsletter? If so, please fill in your name and address.

Name _____

Address _____

City _____ State _____ Zip _____

7378-1